Dragons of Daegonlot

Book Three

The Godling Staff

By Shanlynn Walker

i

Dragons of Daegonlot: Book Three, The Godling Staff

ISBN-13: 978-0997658514 (Shanlynn Walker)

ISBN-10: 0997658517

Written by: Shanlynn Walker

Follow on Twitter: @shanlynnwalker
        Or
On Facebook: www.facebook.com/shanlynnwalker

Cover Design by: Fiverr.com/moonmachine/emmybeks

Contents

Prologue

The midday sunlight streamed down from the sky and illuminated the large black dragon sleeping in a meadow of gently swaying grass. Her onyx scales glittered like priceless black diamonds and the crimson spikes running down her spine shone like garnets, reflecting the sunlight and creating dancing spots of red on the ground around her.

Tucked against her side was an anomaly of grey, also sound asleep with its massive head lying on its front paws which were the size of a human's head. The creature appeared to be a dog, although one of such a size would normally be associated with a horse or some other kind of beast of burden. A falling leaf landed on the beast's nose, gently disturbing its sleep, and suddenly it seemed to fade away, only to reappear solidly, now sleeping on its back with all four feet in the air.

Trakon rubbed his eyes and chuckled quietly to himself. He didn't know if he would ever get used to the sensation of seeing Sylas switch between his ephemeral and corporeal forms. He turned and went back into the cabin. Opening the cupboard, he began picking out vegetables and herbs to add to the pot of dried pork cooking over the fire.

It had been a little over a week since they had returned from their trip into the Myste. They had realized soon after their return that Jessa had somehow come into possession of a staff made from the tree of a godling, and ever since Dax had been trying to find the only godling he knew of; the one that resided on Daegonlot and had fed him as a child. Originally they had planned to travel to Daegonlot the next day, but had decided to let Dax scout ahead to see if he could find the godling. With his newfound powers it was easy for him to teleport and cover more ground alone. So far, however, the search had been in vain.

Absently, Trakon transferred the cut up vegetables into the boiling pot and slowly stirred the contents. He wondered if there was more to Dax's frustration than just the fact he had thus far been unsuccessful in tracking down the godling. His foster parents, Borl and Sikir, also lived on Daegonlot, and Trakon knew Dax had not contacted them since his return from the Myste. It had to be weighing heavily on the young man's mind how they would react to seeing him since his recent transformation. The young man who had entered the Myste had been a blonde-haired, blue-eyed elf with lightly tanned skin kissed by the sun, but that is not who had returned. He had been changed, merged into the being they now knew as Malitak, a creature created and enslaved by the Myste. The Daxon who had emerged from the Myste was paler, and his blonde hair now trailed down his spine, hiding a row of sharp quills. His fingernails were now sharp talons, and his previously blunt teeth now held more than a hint of sharpness, but his blue eyes were still the same.

As if on cue, a roiling, dark grey cloud of smoke swirled into existence and suddenly Dax was standing in the middle of the small living area, cursing. "I've looked everywhere, Trakon," he said without preamble, popping a piece of cut up carrot into his mouth. He swallowed and said, "I don't know what else to do. I've scoured every inch of the island and I haven't seen any sign of the godling. Maybe it doesn't live there anymore..." he said thoughtfully.

Trakon sighed and considered telling Dax his idea. He had been thinking on it for the past few days and had begun to think maybe the godling didn't want to be found. "You know," he began reluctantly, "I've been giving this some thought and maybe I should go with you the next time you search."

Dax looked at him blankly and gestured for him to go on.

"Well, it's possible the godling doesn't want to be found, and I just thought that since I can channel earth magic, I might be able to tell where the largest concentration is, which, hopefully, would be where the godling is," he explained.

Dax looked thoughtful, considering it.

It's a good idea, Drakthira said from outside. *Perhaps we should all go, just in case.*

Silently, Trakon agreed. Dax was ideal for scouting alone since he could simply teleport away from any danger. He could teleport with Trakon as well, but he had to be touching him, and Trakon could imagine all sorts of scenarios where that wouldn't be possible and they may well end up in a dangerous situation. If there were any possibility of that happening, he would prefer to have them all together to face it.

"Agreed," Dax said after a moment of contemplation. "I will teleport us all there tonight after we eat supper. We can get an early start in the morning."

They all agreed and Trakon went to pack the rest of their dried meat and various other foodstuffs in a small pack, along with some basic supplies including rope, a knife, a skillet, and a heavy cloak for himself. When he was finished packing, the stew was done and he and Dax sat down to eat. Sylas had caught a large stag, which he happily shared with 'Thira.

Each of them ate in silence, their minds wandering back to their recent trip through the Myste. Although none of them would admit it out loud, they hoped this trip would be less dangerous, but none of them wavered in their determination to see it through. When they were finished, Trakon took his and Dax's bowl, washed them in the small stream, and strapped their small pack of provisions on Sylas' back. Straightening, he looked at Dax and nodded.

Without a word, Dax climbed atop Drakthira's back and rested his left hand on Sylas' head and clasped Trakon's forearm with his right hand. A column of dark, churning fog surrounded the small party and, when it cleared, the cabin and surrounding meadow were empty.

Chapter One

The traveler was active; he went strenuously in search of people, of adventure, of experience. The tourist is passive; he expects interesting things to happen to him. He goes 'sight-seeing.'

~ Daniel J. Boorstin

Trakon stared off to the east. He could feel an intense pull of immensely powerful magic coming from that direction. Past experience told him that this could mean a variety of things. It could be a large field of trees, plants and flowers raising their arms to the sun and channeling the energy into life; or possibly a recent death, the life energy escaping from the corpse and feeding the earth and animals around it. For that matter, it could also be a newly born litter of some sort of animal just experiencing the first breath of life.

He sighed in frustration and turned, looking to the northwest. Something strangely unfamiliar, partially obscured from his vision, was pulling him from that direction as well. It was odd being lured in two directions at once, but Trakon felt the strongest urge to go east.

He glanced at the other members of his party as they lay sleeping. He had taken the last watch once they arrived on Daegonlot the day before so he could get his bearings and, hopefully, lead them to the godling. It was time to wake them and get started on their journey. With a last look to the northwest, he pulled a skillet out of one of their packs and set it on a large stone that had been warming in the fire and set about making breakfast for himself and Dax. It wasn't long before the noise awakened the others.

Dax yawned and disappeared in a cloud of smoke only to reappear a few feet away, standing now and packing up his bedroll. Sylas, obviously thinking this some sort of new game between the two of them, also disappeared and when he reappeared he had the other end of the bedroll in his mouth and nearly tugged Dax off his feet as he tried to run off with it. In his surprise Dax lost his hold and began chasing after Sylas, shouting for him to bring it back.

Trakon laughed uproariously as he watched Dax teleport in a puff of fog in front of Sylas, who instantly dissipated, dropping the bedroll. Cursing the playful dog, Dax bent to pick it up, but at the last moment Sylas reappeared behind him and, sticking his head through Daxon's legs, snatched the bedroll away. Dax spun around, shaking his fist at the feisty dog, but even he couldn't help but laugh at the huge dog's antics. The two disappeared once more in the smoke, and when they reappeared, Trakon saw that Dax was draped around Sylas' neck, clutching the bedroll in his hand, trying to wrest it from the dog's mouth. Sylas dissipated again, surprising Dax, and both he and the bedroll landed on the ground. Dax stood and brushed off himself and the bedroll, still cursing Sylas, but grinning all the while.

After breakfast Dax and Trakon packed up their belongings and strapped them securely to Sylas. Straightening, Daxon looked at Trakon and asked, "Which way do you think?"

The old man hesitated for just a moment before answering, "Northwest."

After the word was out of his mouth it felt… right somehow. Up to that point he thought he would lead the party east and had surprised even himself. With a last look to the east, he firmly turned himself northwest and began walking, the others falling in line behind him.

The first day passed uneventfully for the party. They stopped at midday and ate some dried fruit and meat and refilled their water from a nearby stream, then started on their way again. Although he knew this was the right direction, by the time they made camp that evening Trakon didn't feel they had come any closer to the mysterious magic calling to him. He began to doubt his decision to come this way, but still felt in his heart it was what they were looking for.

Rising early the next morning, Trakon asked Drakthira if she would mind flying with him for a while. He wasn't worried about Sylas and Dax being able to keep up and he wanted to cover more distance. *I can carry you, dragonrider, but tonight I will have to eat to replenish my strength*, she answered him. He nodded his understanding and Dax, having overheard the conversation, assured her he would hunt for her once they set up camp. He, too, was eager to find the godling, and covering the distance faster meant they would find it sooner rather than later.

Trakon climbed aboard 'Thira's back and with a mighty leap she snapped open her wings, catching a passing current of wind and soared higher into the skies. He was once more overcome with exhilaration as he watched the ground grow smaller and smaller, remembering his flights with Rakisa so long ago. A tear escaped and was swept away by the wind before anyone noticed it, for which he was grateful. That momentary, painful reminder of his lost dragon companion reinforced his determination to discover what was hidden from him ahead, and reminded him of the importance of this quest.

By the end of the second day, their destination still seemed no closer than it was the day before. The island wasn't very large and Trakon knew they wouldn't be able to fly another day without reaching the edge. It suddenly occurred to him that, although he could feel the magic that had beckoned him, it still remained somewhat obscure, as if in the shadows. He began to think that no matter how long they traveled northwest, the magic would still be as far away as it felt now.

As the others settled down, Trakon contemplated a more serious course of action while Dax excused himself to go hunt for

Sylas and Drakthira. He patted Sylas on the head when the big dog jumped up to accompany him, but firmly asked him to stay.

Trakon found a secluded spot not too far from the campsite and settled himself into the tall grass and exhaled loudly, trying to purge his mind of anything and everything, and simply be as one with his surroundings. He closed his eyes and breathed deeply, and simply listened. At first he didn't hear or feel anything, but as he continued to focus on the world around him he began to hear stirrings of life.

Not more than a few feet from where he sat a strange, green and purple bug resembling a cricket began to trill out its nighttime cadence, a sound both beautiful and eerie. Directly in front of him, Trakon could feel the burst of life magic as a small, rodent-like creature gave birth to seven babies in a small den deep within the earth. The old man let his mind touch briefly on the newborn babies, feeling their thirst and the warmth of their mother's body, before allowing his mind to seep into the earth itself, the lush, loamy soil teeming with tiny lifeforms and life-giving nutrients. He followed a system of roots back to the surface, emerging within a small sapling and slowly growing, feeling life as the sapling did, slow and immutable, before finding himself outside of the tree.

His awareness expanding even more, he was now able to make out the smallest motes of magic coursing through the air, following the most miniscule currents. He allowed himself to rise into the air, looking down on the earth from a great height. When he thought he was high enough, he turned his awareness to the northwest, toward the mysterious magic calling out to him, yet remaining hidden. He followed the motes of magic, allowing the air currents to sweep him ever so gently towards a shimmering darkness that for some reason now didn't seem that far away.

He bumped lightly into the shimmering barrier, seeing the motes of magic continue on their way through the shield. He expanded his awareness more than he ever had before, now trying to imagine himself as nothing more than one of the tiny wisps of life and barely able to hold onto his conscious self in such a simple state. Losing himself to his magic, he was finally able to pass through the barrier and continued along with the magic, now more a collection of magical specks than a man. He floated along until, finally, he entered a clearing where the sun shone brightly at its zenith, beaming down on the most beautiful ancient tree he had ever encountered.

Struggling to retain even the small amount of identity left to him, Trakon focused and brought his awareness back together with great effort. The tree before him was massive, even more so than the Whisperwood's tree. Large streamers of moss hung from its branches and leaves in every shade of green imaginable decorated its limbs. The trunk was coarse and in varying shades of brown, from the rich, earthen brown of newly-turned earth to the light, creamy beige of a freshly-cracked nut.

The particles of magic he had followed were swirling around the clearing, but what surprised Trakon the most and captured his attention was the stickman, who wandered around the tree, gently pulling up weeds from around the base of the massive behemoth and stroking its trunk lovingly. Trakon had heard the story of Daxon's childhood benefactor from both Dax and Drakthira, but seeing the stickman himself was an entirely new experience. He watched as the little man picked up a small pail that looked to be made of pure silver, and handed it to a large stag, who took its handle in its mouth and trotted away to a stream Trakon could scarcely make out in the distance.

The little twiggy guy (girl?) then raised its hands into the air and the bits of magic began to coalesce around him. Trakon, too, was gathered along with the mystical specks as they gently swirled in circles around the stick creature. The feeling of being entirely controlled by another being caught Trakon completely off-guard, causing him to panic to the point that his awareness abruptly began to pull itself back together as it struggled to release itself from the stickman's hold and re-enter Trakon's waiting body. As Trakon made his move to escape the clearing, he felt a tremendous force close around him, preventing him from fleeing further. The mysterious force tightened its grip until darkness began to surround him. With one last burst of energy, Trakon telepathically summoned, "SYLAS! HELP ME!"

Daxon teleported back to camp with a broski he had recently killed. Somewhere between a bear and a porcupine, the broski was large and covered with thick fur that hid a collection of quills. It mostly ate an assortment of flowers and berries, but occasionally had been known to scavenge meat, and made a fearsome opponent. Fortunately, Dax had seen the creature before it became aware of him, and had stolen its life-force before it could do much more than turn around. It was large enough to feed both Sylas and Drakthira, so he had quickly taken down a few rabbits for himself and Trakon before returning to camp. Ever since he had realized his ability to teleport, which was just a few days after returning from the Myste, hunting had become much easier. Now he could take down prey of any size and not have to wait for 'Thira to come help him carry it back.

'Thira sent her thanks through their bond before tucking into the broski. Sylas, always eager to show his affection, dissipated and swirled around Dax before his head alone became solid and he planted a large, canine kiss across Daxon's face. Then he joined his dragon friend and together they quickly devoured the five hundred pound carcass.

Dax wiped the dog drool from his face, grinning as he did so. When he had first met Sylas, he hadn't known what to think of the huge dog, and he had neither liked nor trusted either him or Trakon. Now, however, he knew he could trust them with his life, and in fact, had done just that while in the Myste. He held the old dragonrider in the highest regard, and although Sylas sometimes annoyed him, he knew he meant no harm. Secretly he admired the dog. Those who hadn't spent any time with him would think he was just a large, goofy dog, but Dax knew better. He had seen Sylas risk his life for Trakon and plunge fearlessly into danger without a thought for his own safety. Incredibly dangerous, yet retaining an innocence and affection for others, the dog had all the good qualities you would normally associate with a person: love, loyalty, and bravery without end.

Dax was brought out from his reverie by a slight feeling of jealousy coming through from Drakthira. *I am all of those things, too, you know,* she huffed. Dax laughed out loud before answering her, *Yes, you are all those things and more, 'Thira. Nothing compares to you in my book.*

Mollified, the dragon sent a warm wave of affection at Dax, then went back to napping as she normally did after such a large meal. Sylas was snuggled up with her, as usual, but Dax didn't see Trakon anywhere.

Where is Trakon? he asked Drakthira before she could sink fully into sleep.

He went off to meditate, she said drowsily.

Satisfied, he picked up the rabbits he had brought for their dinner and set about skinning them. Once that was finished, he made a makeshift spit, stretching the carcasses out over the built up

8

fire and turning them slowly so they would cook evenly. He stared into the fire as he turned the spit, reflecting on how good it felt to be back on Daegonlot. Although he was aware he used to be two separate entities, only one of which considered this floating island home, he knew he would always consider Daegonlot his home. *To be fair,* he thought, *the Myste is the last place anything or anyone would want to think of as home.*

He looked over at Sylas and wondered how long the dog could remain away from the Myste. As Malitak he had created an internal system in himself that allowed him to be away from the abyss for a time, but he had a feeling the godling they were currently searching for had had a hand in that as well. He didn't know exactly what the being had done to him, perhaps it had made the system he had created permanent somehow, or maybe it would have worked anyway. The truth was, he didn't know. But one thing he did know was that he felt better having the dog around, and wanted to find some way to ensure that Sylas wouldn't have to return to the Myste. He hoped when they found the godling it would be able to do for Sylas what it had done for him all those years ago.

Reminiscing about the time when he was a lost little boy in the forest of Daegonlot made him think of Borl and Sikir, his adoptive parents. As always, when he thought of them, he wondered what they would think of him now. He was no longer the Dax they knew, the carefree youth hell-bent on righting an ancient wrong and protecting the wild dragon hatchling in his charge. Now he knew he was much older than either of them, and at least part of him was a predatory creature from the Myste who had been determined to lead a dragon back to its master, who would then steal its magic. Such polar opposites, and the new Dax had ended up somewhere in the middle. He wasn't sure himself where exactly he had landed on this new spectrum.

9

It crossed his mind to never return to see his parents, but he quickly dismissed that thought. He loved and respected them too much to do that. He couldn't imagine what it would be like to be a parent and not know what happened to your child, to know only that the child had disappeared one day and never came back. No, Dax wouldn't put them through that. They might reject this new Dax, but he would at least give them that opportunity. He would tell them what had happened, as much as he himself understood, and let them decide for themselves. If they didn't accept Dax for who he truly was, at least they would know the truth and avoid spending the rest of their lives worrying over him. He didn't allow himself to dwell on the hurt and disappointment he would feel if they didn't accept him.

Seeing the rabbits were now done, Dax removed them from the spit and laid them to the side to cool. He thought about going in search of Trakon, but hesitated to interrupt his meditations. Hopefully he would come back with some new inspiration as to how to find the elusive godling.

From the corner of his eye he saw Sylas jump to his feet, dissipate, and soar away a split second before the words "HELP! SYLAS!!" thundered through his mind with such force it felt as though his head was splitting in two. Vaguely he heard 'Thira roar, the sound reverberating through the ground and causing their surroundings to quake.

He forced himself to focus through the pain, emitting small tendrils of roiling black smoke to search for Trakon, whose voice he had recognized. Within moments he had found the old man's body sitting prone a short distance from camp. He teleported to the area and instantly realized that Trakon's body was here, but his essence was not.

He placed a hand on the man's body and teleported them both to Drakthira's back just as she sprang into the air. *Can you find him, 'Thira?*

Yes, she answered back after a short pause. *I can track where the voice came from, and Trakon's essence is still tied to his body, although barely. I can see it but it's... hidden somehow. Cloaked. But not for long,* she said determinedly. Dax saw small tendrils of smoke curling from her nostrils and understood. Dragonfire could burn through just about anything. He secured Trakon's body to 'Thira's back, then jumped off, becoming *dim* and soaring through the air above her to stay out of range of her deadly fire.

Chapter Two

While all deception requires secrecy, all secrecy is not meant to deceive.

~ Sissela Bok

Trakon regained consciousness slowly, still somewhat disoriented. As the cobwebs in his mind began to clear, he realized he was looking down at the ground from a great distance. Fear that he was falling washed through him, but as he peered to the left he came to understand that he was actually caught in what appeared to be a giant spider web suspended from high in the huge tree.

Looking all around, Trakon saw no sign of the spider, but he thought it must be huge to have spun a web of this size and strength. He remembered that this part of him was separated from his body and wondered how he came to be caught in a web in the first place. As panic began to set in, he once more speculated on how long he had been gone from his physical self. His body would still be sitting a short distance from the camp, vulnerable… empty.

Hearing a sound below him and looking down, he saw the angry stickman shaking its little twiggy fist at him while jumping up and down in gross agitation. He tried to turn his awareness toward the sun so he could get an idea of how much time had passed while he was unconscious, but whatever was holding his essence here held him fast. He studied the substance as closely as he could, considering his awkward position, and saw that it wasn't a physical web as he had first thought, but rather a web composed of slightly glowing strands of magic.

Trakon no longer heard the stickman hopping below him, and realized everything had gone very quiet. He dared to glance downward once more, and to his dismay he noticed the stickman was very still, staring upward and to the right of Trakon. Turning his head to see the object of the stickman's attention, dread coursed through him. Coming towards Trakon was a huge spider that seemed to be made of the same pasty substance as the web which held him. He could see its ethereal mandibles working, preparing for the meal it was about to receive.

The webbing shook slightly as the spider stepped onto the first strand, the disturbance heightening Trakon's fear to new levels. Every detail seemed clear, and he could make out the bristly hairs on the spider's legs as well as the absence of life in each of the eight eyes. Its fat, luminescent body gave off a dim, green light and Trakon was able to see through the bulbous abdomen.

All too soon he felt the creature's leg brush against him. He struggled as hard as he could, but for all his effort, he only managed to become more entrenched within the webbing. He wished himself to be back in his body so he could at least shut his eyes against the terrible visage of the hungry spider about to feed on his essence. He thought of his friends, Dax and Drakthira, and his ever faithful companion, Sylas, and hoped they would be able to complete the quest they had set out to do without him.

Just as his hope was completely diminished, Sylas suddenly materialized on top of the spider, in full attack. His canine paws clung to the creature's sides, and his massive jaws bore down on the apex between its abdomen and head. The spider shrieked hideously in pain, trying to turn and face its attacker, but the dog's weight overcame any effort the spider attempted. Sylas gave a final, savage twist with his jaws and the spider's head was now dangling by a scrap of skin and mucous. The shrieking abruptly ceased and Sylas jumped clear just as the body of the arachnid fell from the tree to land with a sickening thump on the ground below.

Relief washed through Trakon, but he was still caught in the webbing. When he saw Sylas start towards him, he called for him to stop, fearing the dog would end up entangled in the magical trap as well. Sylas obeyed, but he kept to the upper branches just above where Trakon lay trapped, keeping an eye on the old man to protect him against any more spider attacks.

Shortly after the spider was defeated, a deafening roar shook the clearing, the sound strong enough to cause many leaves to shake loose from their branches and drift to the ground below. The stickman cowered in fear, no longer hopping around and shaking its fist at Trakon and Sylas. The dog looked up to the sky, his stub of a tail making his whole rear end shake in greeting. He watched as white-hot dragonfire burned through the shimmering barrier, the flames licking around the edge and causing them to curl back under the tremendous heat. When the hole was large enough, Drakthira soared through with Trakon's prone body strapped to her back, and landed directly below the old man and beside the still cowering stickman.

The barrier began to repair itself as soon as the onslaught of fire ceased, but before it could close completely, Dax, too, soared through the hole and landed in the tree beside Sylas. He took in Trakon's predicament before gingerly reaching out a hand, palm out, towards the webbing. Like he had done with living creatures before, he willed himself to absorb the life magic within the web, and mote by mote it slowly drained the energy from the trap until Trakon was able to free himself.

Seeing his body atop Drakthira, Trakon's essence soared into it quickly before any other distractions could keep him from returning. Feeling the flesh surround his essence was like coming home, only of a more personal nature. He seldom allowed himself to perform such out of body exploration due to the dangers involved, and judging by this experience, he doubted he would be doing it again any time soon.

Trakon opened his eyes and carefully climbed down from 'Thira's back. Sylas leaped down from the tree and stood beside him, watching to make sure he was alright. Trakon patted the loyal dog on the head, murmuring assurances. He looked around for the stickman who had caused him all this trouble and found him facing off against Drakthira. The dragon had flames flickering around her snout and looked ready to burn the little guy like a pile of firewood, while the stickman cowered in front of her with his little wooden arms set protectively over his head. In an instant a shriek was heard coming from the sky, and when Trakon turned to the source of the scream, a huge phoenix appeared, descending toward 'Thira, its immense talons fully extended!

The flaming bird was slightly larger than the dragon, who roared a challenge at the incoming foe, her spikes standing at attention and protective eyelids descending over her vulnerable amethyst orbs. The phoenix didn't stop or even slow down, crashing into the dragon and tumbling end over end, locked in a deadly embrace.

Trakon saw 'Thira bite down on the bird's neck while the phoenix, who was much more agile than the dragon, tried to blind its opponent with its razor sharp beak. If not for the bony eyeridges above her eyes, the dragon would have already been blinded. Drakthira was mostly immune to the phoenix' fire, but so was it to her's, so a battle of teeth and claws raged across the clearing. Each time 'Thira wounded the phoenix its fire would instantly cauterize the wound, and not even a drop of blood was spilled to the ground, while the phoenix had yet to be able to penetrate the dragon's scaly armor.

The old dragonrider wondered how they were not setting the entire place on fire, but the thought soon left his mind as a silvery steed of moonlight and ferocious beauty charged out of the surrounding brush straight at him. He couldn't do much more than stare at such a fantastic spectacle as the unicorn ran straight at him, its horn lowered to impale him, and its cloven hooves churning up huge tufts of grass and dirt.

Fortunately for the old man, Sylas was not as awestruck as he was, and before the deadly unicorn could thrust its horn through the dragonrider, the huge dog lunged and knocked it down on its back, grasping its neck in his huge jaws. The unicorn reared up in rage and fell straight back. To keep from being crushed to death, Sylas dissipated, and, retaining his misty form, surrounded the mythical creature in a greyish green cloud.

Blisters formed instantly all over the beautiful creature's back and sides, but the poison did not eat through the flesh as it would have a lesser foe. Still, the unicorn was not completely immune and Sylas was rewarded with a scream of pain and rage. The beast kicked out at him, which did little to the dog in his dim form. Sylas maintained his poisonous cloud form to keep the creature's attention on him and diverted from the old man.

Dax saw the fighting unfold below him within a matter of minutes. He was worried for Drakthira and wanted to help her, but he instinctively knew the phoenix fire would also kill him as easily as 'Thira's dragonfire. Seeing that Sylas had the unicorn well in hand, Dax circled the fighting dragon, watching and waiting for an opportunity to help his bond mate. His chance never came, however, for 'Thira finally subdued the giant, flaming bird, pinning its head and wings to the ground and roaring out her triumph.

Dax turned his attention back to Sylas and the unicorn, and, seeing his chance, teleported closer to the two and flung his arms out towards the beautiful, living moonlight. Two quills separated from his back and flew toward the steed, their aim true, burying themselves in the beast's chest.

"STOP!" Dax heard a voice say before everything seemed to slow until, finally, the world stood still.

Drakthira felt a moment of sluggishness roll across her body, but with a growl she shook it off and looked around. The phoenix lay unmoving beneath her, even its flames caught in stasis. Dax was still standing as he had been, slightly bent at the waist, his arms flung forward. His hair, which usually hid the sharp quills along his spine, was still sticking out from where the quills had separated from his body and struck the unicorn. Trakon was standing, wide-eyed, in the center of the clearing under the huge, old tree. The unicorn was still standing although its legs were just beginning to buckle from the wounds in its chest. Even Sylas, still in his poisonous mist form, hung suspended in the air, green sparkles of magic caught in a tiny thunderstorm within his ephemeral form.

Catching movement out of the corner of her eye, 'Thira turned to face this new foe. The creature before her was ever-changing, although in small, minute ways. It jumped from the branches of the tree, its hind legs like those of a large, predatory cat, golden in color with small, black spots on them. It stood upright, like a person, and where the fur ended on its abdomen, a set of iridescent scales took over on its stomach and led up to its neck. The head most resembled a deer, but with a flattened quality, as though it were part human or elf. It had large ears like a deer, and giant antlers rising from its skull. When it turned to regard the fallen unicorn, 'Thira saw it had mossy green fur going down its back, ending in a plush, red tail like a fox.

The being knelt beside the unicorn, waving its muscular arms, which were covered in dense, brown fur, at Sylas, who moved away from the beast, unharmed. Its hands, which 'Thira was sure had been large and tipped with talons, suddenly were small and nimble as they grasped the quills, one at a time, and removed them from the unicorn's chest. It carefully placed both quills in a pouch tied at its waist.

Cupping its hands over the wounds, the creature, whose face now resembled that of an eagle or some other bird of prey, began to chant quietly, and Drakthira saw a green glow coming from its hands. When it removed them a few minutes later, there was no trace of the wounds. Even the fur had grown back, leaving no hint of the previous battle.

When it was finished the creature stood, now on legs covered with black fur that had white stripes running through it, and turned to face the dragon.

"No blood must be spilled in the Grove," it said.

What have you done with my friends? Drakthira asked.

"I have not harmed them, dragon. Come, let's talk. Why are you here? Why do you seek me out?"

You are the godling, Drakthira said, a statement, not a question, but the being nodded anyway. *Then you should recognize your magic,* she said, looking at Daxon.

The godling walked over to Dax and looked him over, peering for a long moment into the frozen man's eyes.

"Yes," he said slowly. "Some of this is my work although it looks like the being that came from the Myste has rejoined the boy I created."

Yes, Drakthira said, not bothering to hide it. *Was that not the intention?*

The godling regarded her for a long moment, unspeaking. Finally, it said, "I could not erase the creature entirely from the boy. The Myste is strong, as I'm sure you are aware. There are many kinds of magic on Darkenfel, mine is but one. The Myste is another. Your kind, yet another."

Yes, but why help the boy? Death is a part of life. Why try to save him?

19

"Oh I didn't save him, not really. I knew what he was. The earth, however... it spoke to me that day, bid me to do what I did. We all come from the earth, you see, all life. It is, therefore, worth listening to it... when it bothers to speak."

What did it tell you? Drakthira asked, curiously.

"If you want to know the secrets of the earth you must ask it. And, if you want the earth to answer you, you must prove yourself worthy of such knowledge," the godling answered cryptically.

Drakthira didn't reply, but regarded the godling out of the corner of her eye. She saw the little stickman, the only other thing moving in the Grove, walk over to the godling and sit beside it.

And the staff you gave Jessa? Did the earth tell you to do that as well?

The godling's face clouded over and for a moment 'Thira wondered if it would attack her. After a few minutes, however, it seemed to bring itself back under control and merely sighed in frustration.

"Come. I will release your friends. Please tell them to leave the other creatures alone, they will not attack again. Then we can discuss the staff," he said, rising.

Wait, Drakthira said, looking around. *Why am I not frozen like the others?*

The godling barked out a short laugh, then shrugged. "Dragons are different," he said. "No being has power over them, not me, not the Myste, not anything. You live on a different plane that simply overlaps this one, but is still removed. No one really knows why, but the Creator must have wanted it that way."

He nodded toward the unicorn and said, "Unicorns are magical creatures, as is the phoenix. Much like dragons, but dragons are more sentient, possessing a noble spirit, great intelligence, and the ability to recognize the same traits in other lifeforms. Unicorns are also very intelligent and noble, but think of them more as nature incarnate. They are fiercely loyal to the earth, but also very wild, driven more by instinct. They love, but they are incapable of empathy. They would never be able to bond with another creature."

He pointed toward the phoenix. "Same for the phoenix, although it's driven more by an all-consuming passion. Fire suits its nature. Everything a phoenix does, it does out of a consuming need to do so. To mate. To fight. To live, and even to die. It has no room in its nature for compassion."

He snapped his fingers and all seemed to be restored to their pre-petrified state. To the others in the Grove, the last thing they remembered happening was hearing the godling shout "STOP!" and all eyes turned his way. By their collective looks of confusion, they didn't understand why he was no longer where he had been when they had been rendered immobile.

Unperturbed, the godling walked to the unicorn and rested a hand on its neck. "Go, my friend," he said, stroking it gently. "There is nothing more to do here."

The unicorn reared up on its hind legs and pawed at the air, snorting, before turning and disappearing into the brush. The phoenix, finding itself no longer pinned to the ground, also took to the air and flew away until the party couldn't distinguish it from the sunlight.

"Now," said the godling, "let's talk."

The godling took a seat on the ground and gestured for the group to do the same. The party hesitated, still unsure exactly what had transpired, until Dax walked purposefully forward and seated himself in front of the godling. The others did the same, forming a small semi-circle around the strange creature.

"So," the godling began when no one else spoke up, "your dragon friend here tells me you are here about the staff Jessa Dragonheart took from me."

"Took from you?" Dax asked. "How did she take it from you?"

"To understand that you would have to understand the world of Darkenfel, and that is not my story to tell. Her secrets are her own."

Trakon spoke up and said, "I'm sorry, Mr…?"

The godling laughed, his face currently looking like that of a feline and the laugh sounding more like a cross between a purr and a growl. "You can call me Aarlian."

"Ok, Aarlian," Trakon began again, "we are on a quest to free the captive dragons Jessa Dragonheart has trapped within an Orb. We sought you out for help having realized the staff she possessed had come from a godling tree, but instead of helping us, you first try to kill me, have your various friends attack us, and now refuse to talk to us, citing you would be sharing some sort of secret of the earth. What, exactly, can you tell us?" he finished in a huff.

Aarlian had the decency to look ashamed and answered the old man. "I'm sorry about your less than warm welcome. You broke through the barrier meant to keep out intruders, and I was fast asleep when it happened. Fortunately I awoke when I did, before blood was spilled in the sacred Grove, but I admit, my golem did take things a bit too far." He looked over at the stickman as he said this, who hung its head in shame.

"But we did spill blood," Trakon said. "Sylas killed the spider."

"Oh, yes, but the spider was made of magic, and wasn't truly alive. Besides," the godling added, "magic never truly dies, it's merely transformed into a different sort of energy."

"So how can we learn about Jessa and the staff?" Dax asked, bringing everyone back to the reason they were here in the first place.

"First you must understand Darkenfel and the creatures in it. What they are, what their purpose is, and how they fit in the greater scheme of things. That includes each of you," he said, holding up a hand to silence Dax when he tried to interrupt. "Yes, young man, I know it sounds like a lot of rubbish to you. You think you already know all of this simply because you are two people who became one. Two perspectives, one person."

Aarlian laughed, this time his face looked like that of a ram and it came out sounding like a bleat. "Most creatures simply can't look outside themselves to know where they fit. They hold themselves in such high esteem they can't imagine a world without them. It's very few, in fact, who can handle the truth of existence and come away unchanged."

"So you are saying we would have a hard time understanding how vastly unimportant we are in the greater scheme of things?" Dax asked to clarify.

"Oh, no, not at all," said Aarlian. "It takes but a single person to change the course of destiny. That should be apparent. Just look at Jessa."

Dax sighed in frustration, feeling like they were talking in circles. "So, what exactly do I have to do to find out more about Jessa and how she came into possession of your staff?" he asked, enunciating clearly.

"The earth can grant you the knowledge that you seek, but it will ask for knowledge in return. Answer truthfully, and you will be granted the wisdom that you seek. Deceive yourself or each other, and you may never be freed from its grasp."

"What does that even mean?" Dax asked. "Why would I deceive myself?"

When Aarlian didn't answer, Dax asked, "So how do we start?"

"First," the godling began, "you must prove your worth to the earth by answering a question. Look deep within yourselves for the answer, and do not lie. If the earth accepts your answer, this," he gestured to a flat rock sitting before him that Dax was sure hadn't been there before, "will open up and you will be allowed to drink of the earth's blood."

"As appetizing as that sounds," Trakon said, his face reflecting his disgust at drinking anything's blood, "why does the earth care about our answers?"

"You're to be its heroes, are you not?" Aarlian asked, looking each of them in the eye. "Isn't that truly what this is about? Freeing the dragons, bringing magic back to Darkenfel? Reuniting Daegonlot?"

How do you know this, godling? Drakthira asked.

"The earth's secrets may be its own, but no secrets are hidden from it," Aarlian answered.

Is the 'earth' as you call it, the Creator?

The godling paused before answering. "I honestly don't know. But it is alive, and very powerful. All life comes from the earth, and all magic, no matter its form. In death, we return to the earth's embrace. We hide no secrets from it."

Drakthira regarded the godling for a long moment. Finally, she said, *How does this work exactly?*

"There are four of you, so four questions will be answered. I don't know what you will see, nor will I be privy to what you experience," Aarlian explained.

"Will we get to go together?" Dax asked.

"I don't know that either," Aarlian said. "This isn't like you are thinking, where the earth is a wholly sentient being. It's lived as long as any of us, and our ancestors before, back to the dawn of time. Our lifetime is but a moment to such a being. Just think of it as living… slower. It has seen the mountains push themselves into the sky, the seasons change, and the lakes run dry. Yet, it has also witnessed the birth of millions of creatures, from the noble dragons to the lowly field mouse, and remembered them all. Their life. Their death. And everything in between."

Dax and Trakon looked at each other, uncertainty clear on their faces. The idea of being trapped by a semi-sentient god-like being didn't appeal to either of them. Trakon didn't doubt a word the godling said. Having the ability to channel earth magic, he knew firsthand the sheer amount of power hidden in the earth the further from the surface you went. He had never tapped into the magical energy there; it felt too powerful for his body to handle. Too unstable. Too alive.

I will go first, Drakthira said, surprising both Dax and Trakon. *Ask me what you will, godling.*

Chapter Three

What is history but a fable agreed upon?

~ Napoleon Bonaparte

Aarlian regarded Drakthira for a long moment. He appeared to be listening to something no one else in the party could hear. Dax was beginning to get restless and was half convinced this was all a trick of some sort when the godling's eyes began to glow with a strange, white light. The pupils and irises completely disappeared, until the eyes themselves were entirely white and luminescent. From the depths of its being came an unnaturally slow, gravelly voice, "DRAKTHIRA," it boomed out, "DAUGHTER OF THE SKIES AND THE GREAT ONYX DRAOGATHRA. WHAT IS THE HEAVIEST BURDEN YOU CARRY IN YOUR HEART?"

'Thira was slightly taken aback by the use of her mother's name, but was not surprised. She had believed the godling when it said there were no secrets from the earth. From the corner of her eye, she saw Dax, Trakon and Sylas turn their heads to hear her answer. She knew her answer already, but was reluctant to speak it aloud for fear of the hurt it might bring her bond-mate. Although they were bonded, there were things that each of them was bound to keep to themselves in order to prevent the other from having hard feelings over things they simply couldn't change. She had expected a different question, something like 'what is your biggest fear' or some other type of common cliché, and was therefore disappointed by her own short-sightedness. Although unwilling, she knew she would answer, and she just hoped Dax would understand.

She looked the being in its milky white eyes and in a voice strong and clear said, *I know my mother, in her darkest hour and unsure if she would live much longer, used the last of her strength to give me the best chance she possibly could to live. I know from the transference of memories when I was still in my shell she had lived her entire life wild and free, and I know she wanted the same for me. Instead, I chose to stay on Daegonlot, mostly out of necessity as I am still a young dragon. But, now, I choose to stay with Daxon, bonded to him, and in doing so I feel I am betraying my mother's last efforts. Now that I am bonded to a rider, I am no longer considered free or wild and I must adhere to the dragonrider's codes. By bonding, I became the very thing my mother didn't want, the thing she despised. I became tame.*

The eerie white eyes held hers for a moment more before the voice spoke again.

"DRAKTHIRA, DRAGON OF ONYX AND AMETHYST, YOU HAVE ANSWERED TRUTHFULLY, BUT KNOW THIS: NO CREATURE GREAT OR SMALL BECOMES SOMETHING ELSE BASED PURELY ON ANOTHER'S PERCEPTION OF REALITY. YOU MAY DRINK OF ME AND IN DOING SO, SHARE MY KNOWLEDGE."

The rock before the godling split with a loud *crack!* and revealed a small puddle of blood-like fluid.

Filing the message away for future reflection, Drakthira stepped forward and lowered her head to drink from the ruby red substance inside the rock. Almost immediately she began to feel dizzy and her eyes became increasingly heavy. The world around her spun, and in a haze she saw the bright sunlight flash by her, replaced by a complete, inky darkness, before returning to the sunlight once more. This cycle repeated over and over, giving her a feeling of falling and spinning at the same time.

After what seemed like hours, the world stopped churning. She knew instinctively that she had been vaulted miles and miles below the earth's surface, and she could see an immense wall of earth and rock above her. Her kind had spent a great portion of their lives sleeping in deep, mountain caves for eons, so she was not uncomfortable in these surroundings; however, she was curious as to *how* she had come to be there.

'Thira found herself within a massive nondescript chamber with no tunnels. The chamber was empty save for a pool of white, molten lava. The heat radiating from the liquid was more than what she considered comfortable, but her scales were able to reflect a great portion of it away from her body, and she therefore felt no threat from it.

A large, grey hand emerged from the lava, startling her and causing her to jump back from the pool until her back was against the smooth, circular chamber wall. The hand was followed by another, then a head, shoulders, torso, and finally, legs emerged until Drakthira found herself looking at a great, grey stony creature standing well over twenty feet tall.

The creature continued its transformation by sloughing off the remaining lava, and now stood before Drakthira as a giant human-like form. As she watched in awe, moss appeared to grow down the lower part of the face, forming a beard-like growth. Two large diamonds, the size of a grown man's fist, pushed through the rocky head appearing as eyes, and dirt began to cover the being's nether regions. When the transformation was complete, the thing looked like a carving of an old man with heavy, blunt features.

Crudely formed lips jutted out from the rocky structure and it spoke its first words, "Welcome Drakthira."

The voice was no longer amplified, but 'Thira recognized it as the voice that had spoken to her from within the godling in the Grove. It had the same gravelly sound and timbre.

Greetings, Old One, she returned, bowing her head slightly.

"What have you come to ask me?" it inquired, the words slow and drawn out, sounding more like 'whhhhhhhhhhhaaaat haaaaaaaaaave yooooooooooouuuuu coooooooooooooome toooooooooooo aaaaaaaaasssssssssskkkk mmmeeeeeee?'

"Would you know how Daegonlot became separated from Darkenfel? Or perhaps you would like to know what happened to your mother after she left you in Goldspine?" it continued in the same slow, grating voice.

It is common knowledge that Daegonlot was separated from the mainland during the race wars, Drakthira said. When she had volunteered to go first, her plan had been to ask how to free the dragons from the Orb, but now her curiosity was piqued. What had happened to her mother? Was she still alive?

A sound like boulders rolling down a hill came from the being, and Drakthira realized after a moment it was laughing.

"The story of Daegonlot is much more than that, young dragon," it said. "What race is strong enough to perform such a feat? Humans? Elves?" The sound of rolling boulders came again. Evidently this creature found itself highly amusing.

Then you are saying the story of Daegonlot is false, she said, making sure to say it as a statement and not a question. She remembered the godling telling her she would be allowed one question, and she didn't want to waste it on something trivial.

"Many stories passed down through the generations are false. It's one of the ways Darkenfel protects itself. Time," it rambled, obviously getting caught up in the complexities only it seemed to understand, "the greatest illusion of all, yet also a reality. How it muddies the currents as it flows. The elves think the human mages and wizards are responsible for what happened. The humans blame the elves and dwarves, and the dwarves simply don't remember or care. But, the dragons," here it paused, briefly. "They are, perhaps, the ones that should really be blamed..."

Drakthira caught herself before blurting out, *What do you mean?* She instead remained silent, contemplating what she wanted to ask. She didn't think the thing was lying to her, and reuniting Daegonlot was one of the tasks the Whisperwood had said needed to be done to save Darkenfel. Besides, she would be lying to herself if she said she wasn't curious why the dragons might be to blame. Had they separated Daegonlot?

She tried to think back over the memories her mother had of the event, and although she could see bits and pieces, they were fleeting glimpses and seemed faded. She realized with a start that although her mother had been alive during, and possibly present for, many of the events that led up to Daegonlot being ripped from Darkenfel, she didn't know who or what had caused it to happen. Drakthira thought her mother had *thought* she knew, and that had been enough to keep her from digging any deeper into the memories, which were actually quite blurred and confusing, leaving 'Thira with more questions than answers.

And what had the being said about her mother? More than anything Drakthira wanted to know if her mother was still alive. She thought if she were she would have tried to return to her daughter, but 'Thira remembered her mother had been weak and senile when she left her egg to the dragonriders. Was she out there somewhere, lost and alone?

Or maybe she should stick to her original plan of asking how to free the dragons. That is what she and Dax had originally set out to do, and so far this was the only lead they had. She thought on it a moment, then wondered silently if she should instead ask how Jessa took the staff from the godling. That knowledge may prove crucial to undoing what Jessa had done.

Frustrated, but no closer to knowing what her one question should be, 'Thira and the stone man regarded each other in silence for a long moment. She thought back to what the godling had said to them in the Grove; *'The earth can grant you the knowledge that you pursue, but it will ask for knowledge in return. Answer truthfully, and you will be granted the wisdom that you seek. Deceive yourself or each other, and you may never be freed from its grasp.'*

Drakthira had not deceived the earth, and if the godling's words held true, that meant the deity would grant her the knowledge she was seeking. Even though she herself wasn't sure what knowledge she lacked, perhaps the earth was trying to tell her that the story of Daegonlot was what she needed to know in order to continue on her journey and free the dragons. Gaining information on her mother, while intriguing for Drakthira, would most likely only benefit her and would not advance them on their quest. The godling had said they were to prove themselves worthy of being the earth's heroes, and although young, Drakthira knew that squandering her question on herself would not be very heroic.

Making up her mind, she said, *What is the history of Daegonlot and how it became separated from Darkenfel?*

"Good question," the rock man said to her, the diamond eyes glowing white hot. It turned back to the pool of lava, beckoning her forward. "Look, and see the truth."

'Thira approached the pool of glowing white lava and after a final look at the stone man, she turned her gaze to its depths. Slowly a picture came into view, unclear at first, but becoming more distinct with each passing second, as if it were rising up to the surface from below.

She realized she was looking down at Darkenfel from the vantage point of one soaring above, higher than she had ever flown. Darkenfel appeared small as a pebble. She was suddenly racing towards the land at super speed, until Darkenfel now appeared to be the size of a grown dragon. Hurtling downward at uncontrollable speed, 'Thira broke through the atmosphere and gazed at the lush forest below, coming closer and closer. But she was traveling so fast that the ground below was nothing more than a vague impression, rendering her unable to get her bearings.

After a while her momentum slowed, and even though she was still high above the forest below, she was at least able to discern certain objects. But as she gazed upon the ground below, she became acutely aware that something was amiss. And it came to her mind that, despite its unmatched beauty, this planet was totally devoid of animal or human life. No animals dotted the meadows, or drank from the numerous lakes and rivers. No birds sang from the trees; no predators roared out challenges to each other. There was nothing, no sign of life at all except for the trees and vegetation.

Drakthira tried to look past the surface of the water to see if there were even any fish in the lakes or rivers, but before she could focus, the stone man began to speak.

"This is Darkenfel in its first hours. Beautiful. Lush. Unblemished by time or creation."

Once more 'Thira found herself hurtling through time, as if the world were being fast-forwarded to another place on the timeline. When it slowed this time, she saw that the forests and vegetation had almost completely covered the surface of Darkenfel, and in the distance, mountains had begun to push towards the sky. There were still no animals to speak of, but the overabundance of vegetation had accumulated so much life energy, she could see little sparkles of green magic coursing through the air. The planet was thick with it; an accumulation of magic she had never before imagined could exist.

Directly below her, a glowing gate appeared out of nowhere, cutting through the air and into existence with a small *pop*. Two children emerged, one a blonde haired little girl who looked to be about ten years old, with golden skin and silver eyes, dressed in a simple, yet elegant, white gown. The other, a boy of about the same age, with black hair and skin the color of dried blood, and dressed in simple, black armor that covered his torso and upper thighs.

After the two emerged she could see them talking to each other excitedly. She was too far away to hear what they were saying, but the stone man gestured, and the vision zoomed in so that they seemed to be only a few feet away.

"This is perfect, Franklin!" the little girl exclaimed, clapping her hands excitedly. "What a wondrous place!"

The boy bowed before the girl, clearly pleased. "I promised you a place where you could create your fantasies, my lady."

The girl waved her hand at the boy, saying, "How many times must I tell you to call me Alexius when we are alone? There is no need for such formalities now."

The boy smiled, but didn't say anything, and the girl eventually went back to exploring. They walked a short distance to a lake and with a wave of her hand, the girl cleared away a huge swath of overgrown vegetation, exposing a large rock jutting up from the earth. She and the boy sat atop the rock and looked out over their newfound kingdom.

"I believe I will start here, Franklin," she said, gesturing with her arms to encompass their surroundings. As she did so, the ground began to quake and the earth broke apart with a horrendous sound. Drakthira watched as a chasm opened where none had been before, and out of it, mountains rose tall, surrounding the lake and a large swath of forest in all directions.

Before she could do more, the boy held a hand up. "Please, my lady, before you create your masterpiece, allow me to create its guardians. It would not do to leave such a wonder unprotected."

The girl rolled her eyes and laughed. "Frank, there is nothing here. What could possibly threaten them?"

Franklin, obviously used to such admonishments, patiently explained, "I know there is nothing here now, but you can never be too careful with such volumes of magic roaming about. What makes this place ideal can also make it dangerous."

Alexius still looked skeptical, but acceded to his wish with a wave of her hand. The boy seemed deep in thought for a long moment, then stepped forward confidently. "I will make you a guardian never before seen or created. A creature of noble spirit, strong of heart, and with the immovable strength of the ocean. It will fly through the sky, yet be at home on the land as well, and covered in armor nigh invincible. I will make it so it can breathe fire so hot it can destroy almost anything."

As the boy explained his wonderful ideas to the girl, her face lit up with excitement and she laughed in delight, clapping her hands.

Franklin motioned with his hands and a sizeable amount of the glowing green sparks of magic united into a large, loose ball. Cupping his hand to his mouth, he breathed into them, then began shaping them with his hands. When he was finished, the vague outline of a dragon was clearly recognizable, hanging suspended in the air. He tore a small piece from his armor, which upon closer inspection looked to be made of a series of overlapping scales, and tossed it absently at his construct, where it attached and multiplied until it covered the entire body. He made a few more adjustments to the form, giving shape to the spikes running down its back and the horns, then stepped back to admire his work. Seemingly pleased, he opened his palm and a white-hot flame appeared out of thin air, dancing right above his hand. This he grasped and flung toward his creation and it was instantly absorbed into the dragon's armor. Finally, he stepped forward and hurled his newly-created dragon to the ground, where it shattered into four identical pieces.

"Arise, Guardians of Darkenfel, and protect your new home," he said. And as he and Alexius watched, the four shapes began to convert into fully grown dragons, two males and two females.

"They are beautiful," the girl gushed, beaming.

The first male dragon was of the purest white with golden spine spikes and claws, and glowing silver eyes. He reminded Drakthira of Alexius, and she was sure that was the boy's intention.

The second male dragon was of the darkest black and had crimson spine spikes and claws, as well as glowing ruby eyes. This dragon reminded her of Franklin, but also of herself as they shared many similarities in regards to color.

The two female dragons were slightly smaller than their male counterparts. The first, a great blue beauty whose color matched that of the sky, had emerald spine spikes and claws, and glowing green eyes. The other female was a deep, royal purple color, with lighter amethyst scales on her belly and spine spikes, and she had glowing amethyst eyes to match.

The boy clapped his hands and in unison the four dragons spread their wings and launched into the sky, each going in a different direction. The children watched them fly off until they were little more than specks in the sky, and ultimately disappeared altogether.

Once the dragons were gone, the girl looked down into the lake below her and thrust her hands toward it. 'Thira was just close enough to notice how the abundant magic motes rushed to do the girl's bidding. They flowed into the water, and where they touched fish were created, as well as frogs, snakes, turtles, and all manner of aquatic life.

"Do you think I should build them houses, Frank?" the girl asked.

"No," the boy answered her. "How will they learn anything if you give them everything?"

The girl looked undecided for a brief moment more, but then her face cleared and she said, "Yes, of course, you are right. I will create them, give them life, and try to guide them in the right direction. But like all things, they must learn to survive on their own. I can simply provide them the tools."

Unlike when the boy created the dragons, the girl seemed to have little need for physical interaction. With a few waves of her hand and a few stifled giggles, the girl created ten beings. At first they were lifeless, and as they lay on the ground the girl bent over each one and with a few spoken words changed a detail here or there. When she was satisfied, she stood and breathed life into each.

Drakthira recognized the creatures as the ancestors of the fey by their appearance. Over time it had changed some, but most of the characteristics were the same. They had the same slanted eyes that gave them a slightly animal-like appearance, and the same sharpness to their features. The most noticeable difference to Drakthira was the absence of fear and rage. These creatures seemed innocent and harmless.

They gathered around Alexius, shyly touching her hair and dress. The girl spoke softly to them, telling them of their new home. Eventually she arranged them into pairs, one male and one female, and told them they would need to use the resources available to build homes for themselves, or suggested they may be able to find shelter in the caves in the nearby mountains. She and Franklin produced small spears, and spent some time teaching them how to spear fish for food.

They spent the first night with the fey, helping them and teaching them things they would need to know to survive. Drakthira noticed neither Franklin or Alexius performed magic in the vicinity of the fey, and instead used their hands to manually perform mundane tasks like cutting wood and rubbing two pieces together briskly to build a fire.

'Thira wanted to see the dragons again, but they never returned. On the second day, the two children left their creations to fend for themselves, telling them goodbye and promising to return again in the future. Hand in hand they walked away until they were far enough they would not be seen. With a few gestures, the girl created a portal like the one Drakthira had seen them come through originally. Once they walked through it disappeared, leaving not a trace that it had ever been.

Drakthira looked up at the stone man and asked, *How long has it been?*

"Our first jump, when time sped up, was one thousand years. That is how long it took for the magic to overrun Darkenfel and permeate the entire land," he answered.

One thousand years, then the children arrived. They were the Creators. And they made dragons first. Her chest swelled with pride as she said the last.

The stone man laughed. "Yes," he said. "Dragons were the first creatures to ever live on Darkenfel. They were created for a purpose, to protect the land, and did so for a great many years."

Then what happened?

"Watch," he said, once more pointing into the lava.

Time sped by again, reminding 'Thira of the time she was trapped with Daxon inside their joined minds. She watches as the children return sporadically throughout the years, never leaving their creations alone for long. The fey village grows quickly at the increased speed at which she watches, and before long there is a thriving community living together happily.

As more time passes, the children begin to show signs of aging, and Drakthira sees them turn into adolescents, teens, and finally, young adults. Still, they visit periodically, watching over their creations and sometimes bringing them presents or teaching them new skills.

During one of their visits time slowed to normal and 'Thira watched with interest as the two stepped out of their portal. She could tell Alexius was upset, and she appeared to have been crying. Franklin held her in his arms, whispering to her, and Drakthira heard him say, "It's for the best."

They hurried off towards the fey village, hand in hand as they always had before. This time, however, they did not bring gifts or spend time showing their worshippers new skills. They merely sat with them, and blessed them with their affection. After just a few short hours, they got up to leave and hurried back to their world.

Before they stepped through the golden gate, Alexius said, "I will destroy the gate from the other side so no one else can ever come here from our world. They will be all alone, Frank," she said, burying her face in his chest.

He stroked her hair as he held her close, and whispered in her ear, "I know, I know. But it's the only way to keep them safe, to prevent this world from becoming like our own. We have destroyed our universe. Let's not do the same to this one."

Alexius nodded tearfully and they both went through the gate and disappeared, never to be seen on Darkenfel again.

Time speeds up once more and life goes on in the fey village. At first it doesn't appear that anything has changed, but as time goes on, the village begins to fall into disrepair and fights begin to break out among the villagers. Soon the village is deserted, the fey having split up and left to seek somewhere else to call home.

Over time they are spread throughout the borders of Darkenfel, and Drakthira watches as the magic builds and builds until, finally, it begins to react in strange ways. Portals appear out of nowhere and sometimes, before they close, humans emerge.

At first it is a mere handful of human residents, but over time they come together, forming villages and breeding. They start out as non-threatening residents, but over the years the magic of Darkenfel seeps into their offspring and with each generation the power grows stronger within them. Powerful mages, witches, and warlocks finally emerge, bending the magic to their will. Inevitably, as more villages are formed the residents go to war with one another, and the more prominent wielders of magic face off against each other. Entire villages are razed and wiped out.

Drakthira wondered why the dragons don't interfere, but they are as yet still unseen by the humans of Darkenfel.

The fey have continued to breed, and they, too, are being affected by the plethora of magic. Although they do not have strong internal magic like the humans, they have learned to leech magic from their surroundings. Eventually they and the humans clash in a dispute over land and hunting grounds. It is at this point the dragons make themselves known, protecting the fey against the humans and wiping out the village of attackers with their raging fire before disappearing once more.

The fey, worried and frightened over the human's powerful magic, create the Myste to protect themselves and to prevent more human intruders from coming to Darkenfel. For many years this works, and the number of human inhabitants coming through slows to a trickle. The fey are protected from the humans already in residence, as the humans are afraid of the Myste and avoid it at all costs.

The Myste becomes almost a living thing, forming its own kind of magical energy that is slightly different from the magic already infusing Darkenfel. The reactions between the two bring about even stranger and more powerful creations. Over the course of the next few thousand years, unicorns, phoenixes, griffins, and a menagerie of other creatures appear, populating the land.

Dwarves also appear, offspring of lost rock spirits known as mimotans. The mimotans broke off from their mountain homes during the wars as magic blasted the land and decimated mountains. These spirits eventually evolved into the dwarves who took up residence within the mountains, never quite overcoming their affinity for rocks and living underground.

The dragons have also multiplied and now number in the hundreds. Some humans take to hunting them, afraid they will attack their villages or eat their offspring. More wars break out as the dragons fight to protect themselves and the other residents of Darkenfel. From their perspective, the humans are the true invaders, for they have amassed a population large enough to be considered a threat, and they cannot seem to live in harmony with the other residents of Darkenfel. Rather, they form large hunting parties and slaughter unicorns for their alicorns, to use in magic potions or some magical trinkets. Phoenixes are hunted for their feathers, and even dragons are killed for their eyes, horns, scales, and teeth, anything the humans think will make them more powerful.

Drakthira watches, saddened, as the dragons and humans fight each other. The dragons are severely outnumbered, but are more powerful than the humans, able to wipe out entire villages in a single day. The humans, on the other hand, fight at great cost to themselves, taking down one dragon for every hundred humans lost, but with each one destroyed the threat is lessened.

The fey remain in the Myste, unable or unwilling, or possibly just unaware, of the fighting outside their home. They don't help either side. The dwarves remain in their mountains, uncaring about the outside world for the most part. Dragons have nowhere to turn for help, except to the magical creatures of Darkenfel, the ones also being hunted by the humans, but they number even fewer than the dragons, rendering them of little assistance.

Salvation finally comes in the form of a powerful human mage. He stumbles across a dragon mother protecting her eggs, but she has been badly wounded. He takes pity on her and heals her, then stays with her until her eggs hatch. During their time together the two become friends, each seeing in the other similar traits and a noble spirit.

The mage helps her raise her hatchlings for the first year of their life until they are old enough to fly off on their own. Both realize they do not want to leave the other, or rejoin the fighting between the dragons and humans, and together they begin to search for a solution.

Separately, they approach members of their own kind and begin to encourage peace between them. It takes many years, but eventually there is a group of twenty-two dragons and over a hundred humans of like-minded individuals. Finally a promising start to end the war, until the group is betrayed by one of its human members and they are set upon and nearly wiped out by a small army of mages and wizards.

The mage and his dragon friend, realizing they have no hope of winning, devise a solution out of desperation. Harnessing as much magic as he can, the mage tries to save his friends by lifting the very ground they stood upon above the fighting. But he underestimates the amount of magic it will take to accomplish such a feat, and begins to falter before the separation even begins. The dragon, however, realizes the mage's intention, and joins her magic to his, and with combined effort, what is now known as Daegonlot begins to rise into the air.

Unbeknownst to the wizard, the effort has cost the dragon her life, which she willingly sacrifices to save his and the rest of their group. Once he realizes that he has lost his friend forever, he is overcome with grief. He amasses the very last of his magical energy, including his own life energy, to cast a final spell which will hold Daegonlot suspended indefinitely, out of the reach of the humans below.

Neither the humans below nor the now-separated group of humans and dragons on Daegonlot witnessed what caused the rising of Daegonlot, and therefore do not know how the island was created. Each clan blames the other. The bodies of the mage and his dragon friend are hidden away in a small, unknown cave, and are never found. To this day, no one knows of the sacrifice they made in their quest for peace.

Time goes on and eventually all of the dragons end up on Daegonlot, finding it easier to live out of the reach of the humans below. The Daeglonlot humans start their own village, which will come to eventually be known as Goldspine, and the dragons of Daegonlot live in peace alongside them.

How long was that jump? Drakthira asked.

"One hundred thousand years," the stone man replied.

None of those people were dragonriders, she stated.

"No, that didn't come for many more years, but that is another story. Your question has been answered, and you now know how Daegonlot was separated from the mainland," he said.

How does this help me? she asked just as darkness began to close over, and she once more felt like she was spinning away.

As if from a long distance away, she heard him reply, "If you know the *history* of its creation, then you can shape its *future*."

Chapter Four

True love is selfless. It is prepared to sacrifice.

~ Sadhu Vaswani

Drakthira opened her eyes and found herself once more back in the Grove. Dax was looking at her expectantly. *Are you going to ask your question, 'Thira?* he asked.

I already have, she replied. She shared with him all that had transpired and all that she had perceived, opening up the memory for him to see, transferring everything within a matter of moments.

We will need to discuss this with Trakon. Maybe he can help us figure out how to undo the mage's spell on Daegonlot, Dax said thoughtfully. Drakthira sent her agreement before turning back to regard the godling who, up to that point, had not spoken.

"Welcome back, Drakthira," Aarlian said, "I hope you found the knowledge you were seeking."

'Thira bowed her head slightly at the godling, but remained silent.

"Pardon me," Trakon said, leaning forward. "I know you said we could all ask a question, but, do we all have to ask it now? I mean, I don't know yet what Drakthira asked, but perhaps we should get some time to discuss what we have learned before deciding on what to ask next?" he asked, looking around at the rest of the party for agreement.

Aarlian smiled at Trakon. "A wonderfully wise decision," he said, rising. "Please rest here tonight. I will ensure your safety and privacy."

After the godling left the party to themselves, Drakthira shared what she had learned with the others in the group. Daxon, since he already knew what she had discovered, set about making camp. Out of habit he began to make a fire before realizing the sun was still high in the sky and giving off more than enough warmth.

"I don't know what this place is," he started after 'Thira had finished her tale, "but it makes me uncomfortable. I don't think the sun has moved since we entered here."

This isn't a 'place' exactly. It's different, removed from the normal course of time in some way. Here, but also not here, like it has been set atop your reality, but not anchored. I can feel the difference. It's like I'm sitting in a deep pool of a slow-moving stream. The pool remains the same, while the stream moves through it, Drakthira explained.

Trakon, who normally would be brimming with questions over such things, remained unusually quiet. He was thinking over what 'Thira had discovered. He, like most residents of Darkenfel, had always assumed Daegonlot had become separated from the mainland by some sort of magical means, but now knowing how it was accomplished, he had a better understanding of their task, as well as what it would take to accomplish it.

"Magic done requires the same, if not greater, amounts to undo…" he whispered to himself under his breath, remembering a lesson taught to him by his father many years ago. With magic, all things mattered. Not just the ingredients or source of the magic, but all things, even intangible things. The mage who had cast the spell to keep Daegonlot afloat had intended to sacrifice his life to save his friends, and the dragon who had given her life to help had done so willingly. Their selflessness was intangible, but would play a great part in reuniting the island with the mainland. The only way to undo it would be to find another dragon and humanoid willing to give their lives to accomplish the mission, which Trakon dismissed immediately. Even if they approached a dragonrider and his dragon and explained the situation, it wouldn't matter. People were content with how things were and saw no need to reunite Daegonlot. Trakon didn't blame them; on the surface all appeared fine. It was only after traversing through the Myste and hearing the Whisperwood's warning that he understood why it had to be done.

He considered Drakthira and Daxon, but immediately dismissed that thought. Not because they might refuse; oh no, they most likely possessed the courage and determination to succeed where other dragons and their riders would fail. Aside from purely selfish reasons, including the fact that they were his friends and he wanted no harm to befall either of them, who, then, would be left to free the other dragons, including his beloved Rakisa? An old man and his giant dog? Would that even be enough?

No, he thought. *They stand a better chance of freeing the dragons than I do, even with Sylas to help me.*

Another way to undo it would be if the exact opposite were to happen. Suppose, for example, that there were people who wanted Daegonlot rejoined with the mainland for their own selfish reasons, such as destroying once and for all the dragons and their riders. Their fear and hatred would, in effect, cancel out the magic that made the original spell successful, the love and sacrifice. Trakon estimated the chances of this happening were even smaller than approaching another dragon and rider. Few people even remembered the dragons anymore, or the dragonriders, and, what's more, without knowing the details of what the original mage intended, it would be too risky. *Intangibles,* he thought, *the strength and weakness of all spells.*

That left just one possibility. The spell could be reversed with a great source of power, one great enough to tear open the bindings of the original magic by sheer force rather than unraveling them with a counter-spell. This, too, was far from an ideal solution. First of all, Trakon didn't know if such a source of power existed. Dragon magic, part of the original spell, was no easy thing to overcome, and what's more, a spell cast out of love and selflessness was much harder to break than one spoken for evil reasons. Trakon suspected that Daegonlot had remained in its suspended state for so long because the magic used to put it there

49

in the first place came from love and sacrifice rather than hatred and greed.

Trakon pushed these thoughts aside and forced himself back to the present, only to find everyone looking at him.

"Well?" Dax asked, "You've been muttering under your breath for some time now. What did you find out?"

Trakon shook his head. "Nothing, really," he said, "just the ramblings of an old man."

Daxon studied the old dragonrider for a long moment. He wasn't convinced Trakon was telling them everything, but he trusted the old man enough to let it pass. He would tell them in time.

As if he could read Daxon's thoughts, Trakon said, "I will need more time to think on the events of Daegonlot and how we can undo what has been done. For now, I think we should figure out what questions we want to ask, and who should ask them."

Dax nodded his agreement. "There is the obvious; 'how do we free the dragons' question," he said.

Trakon stroked his beard absently. "I'm not so sure that is the obvious question, Dax," he said quietly.

When Daxon raised his eyebrows at him questioningly, he continued, "The question just seems too broad when you think about it, and what if there is more than one way? How would we know what is the best way?"

Very wise, Trakon, Drakthira said. She reflected on her time spent with the stone man, then said, *The earth man offered me a few suggestions, almost as if he were trying to help me. Perhaps asking how to undo isn't the right way. Perhaps it is, as with my vision of Daegonlot, better to ask how it was done.*

"My thoughts exactly, young dragon," Trakon said. "If we know how it was done, we can possibly figure out how to undo it."

"Ok," Daxon said, his tone thoughtful, "then one of the questions should be how Jessa got the staff."

Trakon and Drakthira nodded agreement while Sylas simply emitted a loud snore from the dragon's side where he was curled up asleep. Trakon chuckled at the dog, and Dax grinned.

"I'd also like to ask for the godling to make it so that Sylas never has to return to the Myste," Dax said.

Both Trakon and Drakthira agreed, then Trakon said, "That leaves us with one more question, and, for myself, there are two that I think would be the most valuable. One, how did Jessa create the Dragon Orb? And, two, how did the Orb end up under Daegonlot? Actually, now that I think about it, perhaps a third; is Jessa still alive, and, if so, where is she?"

"Why would that help us?" Dax asked.

"Who better to know how to undo what's been done?" Trakon asked.

"Perhaps," Dax started, "but what makes you think she would tell us even if she were alive and we did find her?"

Trakon didn't answer for a long time and Dax thought the old man had simply ignored his question, but finally, he said, "She wasn't always so... bitter. Maybe part of her still isn't."

"That's a big maybe," Dax said gently, "too big to count on in my opinion."

You two should decide what question you are going to ask and leave the rest alone. You cannot control what Sylas will do, Drakthira suggested.

Trakon barked out a short laugh. "You are quite right, 'Thira," he said. "All the planning in the world won't matter when it comes to Sylas. I'm not sure how he will communicate his question, but I have been around him long enough to know I shouldn't doubt him."

Sylas will have no trouble asking his question. He may not communicate in a way you or Dax understand, but I understand him well enough, and I'm sure the stone man will as well.

"Well, one thing is certain. Sylas will never ask anything for himself. I will take that upon myself Dax, and leave it to you to ask what you think is best in regards to Jessa and the Dragon Orb. Hopefully, between what 'Thira has found out, your question, and whatever Sylas asks, we will have a clear path forward," Trakon said, yawning. He rose to go find a soft patch of grass to rest upon, leaving Dax and Drakthira alone with the snoring Sylas.

They sat in companionable silence for a long time, each lost in their own thoughts. Finally, Dax said, "What did they seem like, 'Thira? The Creators?"

The young dragon thought back on her vision of the two, once more watching them grow up through a series of disjointed images show to her by the stone man.

Innocent, she said at least. *At least at first, when they were children. The ebon-haired boy, my Creator, cared for the girl and seemed to want to protect her.*

"And the girl?" he prodded.

She seemed to want to make something beautiful. Beautiful creations in a beautiful world. Innocent, like herself. She contained them with the mountains, as if she didn't want to claim all of Darkenfel, but just a small portion of it. Perhaps to have room for her creations to expand in the future. She seemed distraught over leaving the last time, she finished.

"Do you think they will ever come back?" Dax asked quietly.

I have no way of knowing such things, but I think they would come back if it were possible.

"Knowing there are Creators is very… unnerving for me. I mean, I know we all think there are Creators, but more in an abstract way. Now, I have seen them through your memories. I know what they look like."

Why is that unnerving? They had to look like something.

"Yes," he said, "but now I also know they didn't 'create' me. The Myste did. Before now, I'd not given much thought to that. But, now that I have, I realize I'm little more than a forgotten wisp of imagination created by a semi-sentient creation of the fey, the true and original inhabitants of Darkenfel. The ones rightly meant to exist. The ones truly crafted by the Creator."

Drakthira didn't know how to respond. She could feel the melancholy thoughts weighing heavily on her bond-mate, but nothing she could say would change Daxon's origins. Finally, she said, *Many of Darkenfel's inhabitants were not directly 'created' but I don't think that makes them less in any way. Besides, we do not know the minds of the Creators. Perhaps this is how it was supposed to happen.*

Dax stretched out on the grass beside her. "Maybe so," he said thoughtfully, before drifting off to sleep.

The small party was once more grouped around the godling in a semi-circle. "Have you thought about your questions?" Aarlian asked them.

Trakon leaned forward. "Yes, and I'd like to go next."

"As you wish," the godling said and closed his eyes.

After a few moments the eyes opened and were once more glowing white. "TRAKON, SON OF TREVAN, YOU ARE NOT OF THIS WORLD. WHAT MAKES YOU WORTHY TO BE A HERO OF DARKENFEL?"

Taken aback by the question, Trakon stammered, "I…I…I…I'm not sure, I…" He took a deep breath and reflected on the question. It was true, he was an outsider from another world, but Darkenfel had been his home for many years. Not only that, but it felt like his home, even more than the world to which he had been born. He had met Jessa here and fallen in love. He had experienced the friendship of a dragon and soared the skies of Darkenfel upon her back, the wind upon his face. He had met Sylas here during his darkest and loneliest hours, finding a companion and friend. Finally, he had found hope in Daxon and Drakthira, hope of finding his lost dragon friend as well as hope for the future of all dragons.

He squared his shoulders and shook off any doubts he had. "I have come to love Darkenfel as my home, even if it is not where I was originally born," he began. "What's more, I am committed to saving the dragons, as well as Darkenfel, but more than that, I also want to save Jessa, another outsider." He saw Daxon's eyes widen in surprise as he said this, but he kept going. "I would find a way for all the residents of Darkenfel to live together in peace, the dragons, humans, myself, Jessa… everyone. There has been enough bloodshed, enough turmoil. It's almost destroyed this beautiful land, and I will do whatever I can to repair what has been done at the hands of humans."

"YOUR WORDS RESONATE THROUGH THE EARTH WITH THE RING OF TRUTH, BUT KNOW THIS: RIGHT AND WRONG IS NOT ALWAYS EASILY DISCERNABLE. YOUR DEDICATION TO DARKENFEL IS ADMIRABLE, YOUR DESIRE TO SAVE YOUR LOST LOVE IS COMMENDABLE, BUT IT IS YET TO BE SEEN IF THEY CAN COEXIST. NOW, WHAT IS YOUR QUESTION?"

Trakon hesitated, pondering the godling's words. Then, he said, "What I seek, what is most important to me, is not knowledge. I'd ask that Sylas be freed from the hold the Myste has on him, able to walk about Darkenfel freely, never having to return to the abyss."

Trakon leaned forward to drink from the blood in the stone, but it remained closed. He looked at the godling questioningly.

The godling hadn't moved. His eyes still glowed with white-hot brilliance, and Trakon could feel them burning into his own as the entity within Aarlian regarded him. "TRAKON OF OUTWORLD, YOU WOULD GIVE UP YOUR QUESTION FOR THIS FAVOR FOR YOUR FRIEND. ARE YOU SURE? KNOWING YOU WILL NEVER AGAIN HAVE THIS OPPORTUNITY?"

"I am sure," Trakon said, no hesitation in his voice. "I truly believe Darkenfel is a better place with Sylas in it. He is noble, brave, and courageous. He should not have to go back to that dark place from which he escaped."

"THE MYSTE SERVES A PURPOSE, AS DO WE ALL," the being answered.

"A purpose Sylas is no longer suited for," Trakon replied smoothly. "When I inadvertently changed him he was freed from the hunger that drives the creatures of the Myste. Not only that, he was shown a different way, and embraced it fully, no longer uncaring and removed, Sylas cares greatly for others and no longer has the desire to kill."

Minutes passed and the godling remained silent. The others simply waited, also not speaking, to hear what the final decision would be. Finally, he said, "I CANNOT CHANGE WHAT SYLAS IS. HE WILL ALWAYS BE A CREATION OF THE MYSTE'S MAGIC. I CAN, HOWEVER, IMBUE MY OWN LIFE-MAGIC INTO THE TETHER HOLDING HIM TO THE MYSTE SO HE WOULD NOT HAVE TO RETURN, HOWEVER, I HAVE NOT YET DECIDED THAT IS APPROPRIATE. YOU CAN EITHER ASK A DIFFERENT QUESTION, OR I WILL MAKE MY DECISION AFTER I HEAR SYLAS' QUESTION. DECIDE."

Trakon didn't need to think it over. He answered, "I will await your decision then, Wise One."

The godling's eyes lost their white glow and once more Aarlian addressed the group. "Do you have another question prepared?"

How did the stone man know? Drakthira asked before anyone else could say anything.

"Know what, young dragon?" the godling asked, confused.

When I was given the opportunity to ask my question, I drank from the stone first. Why did Trakon not have to drink first before asking his question?

"The secrets of the earth are its own," he answered vaguely, "but, as I told you before, we hide nothing from the stone man, as you call him."

"Then I guess my question will not come as any surprise either," Dax said. "And I will go next."

Chapter Five

We have enslaved the rest of the animal creation, and have treated our distant cousins in fur and feathers so badly that beyond doubt, if they were able to formulate a religion, they would depict the Devil in human form.

~ William Ralph Inge

"DAXON AND MALITAK, ONE A SON OF BORL, THE OTHER A CREATURE OF THE MYSTE, BOTH UNITED IN THE BODY BEFORE ME. TELL ME, WHICH ONE TRULY CAME OUT OF THE MYSTE? WHICH ONE IS TRULY MORE DOMINANT SINCE YOU HAVE MERGED?"

Dax started to give the answer he had to his friends when they had first emerged from the Myste, but something stopped him. He looked deep within himself, reflecting on the life of Daxon and Malitak, both together and individually. He would be lying if he said he never had doubts about how much of him now was Malitak.

When he was around his friends, especially Drakthira, he always felt more like Dax than Malitak. It was easier to be Dax, his love for his friends overshadowed Malitak's hunger for their magic easily. But, when he wasn't around his friends, things were not always so clear.

He thought back on the many scouting trips he had taken to Daegonlot in search of the godling. Most had been rather uneventful, but one in particular had left him shaken. He had been walking through a dense forest looking for signs of the ancient tree he remembered from his youth when he happened upon a goriak. By the time he saw the creature it had already spotted him and was nearly upon him. It was huge, an adult male, all claws, dense fur, and fangs as long as his finger. Before he could teleport away, the goriak leaped at him and instinct had immediately taken over. A piercing shriek of challenge had torn from his throat and all fear had melted away. When the fighting was over, the goriak was little more than a steaming pile of meat with patches of fur clinging to it. He remembered going to a nearby pond to clean the blood from himself, and, upon seeing his reflection, he realized at that moment he resembled Malitak more than Dax. His teeth had been elongated and sharp, but most disturbing were his eyes, which had turned black. After a short while he had continued with his search, and by the time he had returned to Trakon's cabin he had dismissed his reflection as a trick of the water.

But now, thinking back, he wasn't so sure. Allowing himself to look deep within, Dax understood that on the surface he appeared to be the Dax that everyone knew, albeit with many of Malitak's magical abilities and some slight physical resemblance to the creature. But, beneath the surface, something darker stirred, and another side that emerged whenever he felt threatened.

Taking a deep breath, Dax met the glowing white orbs and answered, "Malitak and Dax are now one and the same. I, too, have wondered which truly came out of the Myste as sometimes I feel more like Dax and other times I feel more like Malitak. But, how else could it be? I was two beings. Is it not probable that I would be both, given the circumstances and situation? Although I am both Malitak and Daxon joined into one person, I still have the memories of two separate entities, and naturally I draw on the experiences of both. I will admit there is more of Malitak within me than I originally thought, but the hunger that defined him is not present within me. What defines me is my love and devotion to my friends and that comes solely from Daxon. So, to answer your question, one must first define what makes a man. Is it his ability for violence? If so, then I am Malitak, the Reaper, and my ability for violence is great indeed. Or, is it his compassion and empathy for others? If so, then I am Daxon, for I am not ruled by fear or hunger, but by empathy and compassion. My first instinct is not to kill, but to understand."

"YOU SPEAK TRUTH AND WISDOM, AND THEREFORE YOU SHOULD NO LONGER HARBOR ANY DOUBTS ABOUT YOUR IDENTITY. MALITAK WAS NEITHER GOOD NOR EVIL; HE WAS MERELY A GOLEM WITH NO CAPACITY FOR EITHER. LET GO OF YOUR DOUBTS AND EMBRACE THE MAN YOU HAVE

BECOME. YOU MAY NOW DRINK AND SHARE MY
KNOWLEDGE."

Daxon cupped his hand in the red liquid of the rock and
brought it to his lips, drinking deeply. Then the world spiraled out
of control.

When Dax regained consciousness he expected to find
himself in the chamber from Drakthira's memory. He was
pleasantly surprised to find himself standing before a pretty and
serene pond, no more than fifteen feet in diameter. The pond was
located in a shallow cave, and when Dax walked to the entrance he
found he was atop a high cliff overlooking Daegonlot. He turned
back to the pond and was surprised to see an identical pond on the
roof of the small cave, mirroring exactly the one on the floor.
Walking towards the identical pools he gazed into the depths of the
one on the floor and saw Dax staring back at him. Not the current
Dax, but the Dax he used to be, with tanned skin and blonde hair.
Surprised, he raised his hand to feel the thick, blonde hair, but felt
only the hair he now had, which was overlaid with sharp quills. He
also noticed the Dax reflecting back at him in the pool did not
mirror his action as most reflections do, but simply stared back
him.

Raising his eyes, he looked into the pond above him and
saw the reflection of Malitak staring back him. The vision was so
realistic he jumped back and instantly dropped into a defensive
stance upon seeing it, but, again, the image merely stared back at
him, unmoving.

"The Pools of Truth can take some getting used to," said a slow, gravelly voice from behind him. Dax whirled around to see the stone man from Thira's memory standing at the mouth of the cave.

"What would you like to ask of the earth? Perhaps you would like to know the story of Jessa Dragonheart? The true story, of course, and not that fiction they teach in Goldspine. Or would you, perhaps, like to know more of the powers Malitak possessed?"

"I have no need to know of Malitak, Great One," Dax answered respectfully, "I'm sure I will discover any remaining secrets in time if they exist. Show me instead the story of Jessa Dragonheart. Particularly how she managed to create an Orb that could trap the dragons."

"Look, and you shall see," the creature said, his eyes glowing with white fire.

Dax looked into the pool on the floor of the cave. At first, all he could see staring back at him was the reflection of himself in years past, but then a tiny ripple interrupted the smooth surface of the water. He watched as the ripple grew, spreading over the entire body of water. As it passed, the image reflecting back at him changed.

Dax saw that he was no longer visible in the pool's surface, but as he continued to watch, a young woman emerged from a tiny tunnel in an underground cavern. She was soaking wet and shivering with cold. The water surrounding her drew his attention immediately, as it was red in color, and he had never seen any water like it before. He glanced at the pool above him, seeing the same image except now, the water shimmered and sparkled radiantly.

"Why does the water look differently in this pool?" Dax asked the stone man, gesturing towards the pool above him.

"That pool will show you visions through Malitak's eyes, while this pool," he gestured toward the pool in the floor of the cave, "will show you through Daxon's eyes."

Dax nodded his understanding, although he wasn't sure why he needed two separate ways of looking at the same thing.

"The water in the image above is different because Malitak's eyes recognize the magic hidden below its depths," the stone man continued as if reading his mind.

"What is it, and where does it come from?" Dax asked.

"It is called the Blood of the Mountain and it plays a vital role in our story. Watch," he said, once more causing the placid pool to ripple.

Daxon witnessed Jessa's meeting with Riiele, the strange, purple dragon he had met under Daegonlot once before. He watched as they met each other, Riiele in the form of a man, and it didn't escape his notice how desperately Jessa needed his company. It also didn't escape his notice that, over time, as Jessa drank from the ruby waters, they seemed to lose their red luster until, eventually, they were as clear as a mountain spring. Looking into the pool above him, he was taken aback at how much she had changed in Malitak's eyes. Her entire being seemed to glow with a faint, reddish aura that followed her everywhere she went. Tiny thunderstorms of red lightning swept over her being, but neither she nor Riiele seemed to be aware of them.

Time passed, and Dax saw Riiele saying farewell to Jessa as he led her out into the sunlight. Just before she took her final step, tears streaming down her face, she turned and looked back, looking to Dax as if she were hoping for one last glance at her lost love, before she wiped the tears from her eyes and continued out of the cave.

Glancing up, Dax caught a momentary flash of brilliance as one of her shed tears landed on the ground, and Jessa simply disappeared.

"Where did she go?" he asked, squinting at the pool as if it would show him what had happened to the woman.

"To Daegonlot, young rider, or at least what would soon become Daegonlot. It had not yet been separated from the mainland. As Jessa left the cave in the Crimson Peak Mountains, her tear inadvertently opened a portal to Daegonlot and she didn't even notice. She thought when she left she was simply walking out above ground, never aware she had been teleported to another place. At least, not then."

Turning back to the pool, the stone man waved his arm and the image disappeared, to be replaced a moment later with a vision of Daegonlot. Jessa was walking along a stream, looking at everything with a sense of wonder. Dax surmised it must have been shortly after she had left the cave, when the world of Darkenfel was still new to her.

The stone man touched the water with his finger, and time was fast forwarded. Dax saw a much younger Trakon and Jessa meet, and, eventually, fall in love. He witnessed the day Trakon risked his life to save Rakisa's hatchling, and the beginning of their friendship. "He really was the first dragon rider," Dax mumbled to himself.

"Yes, Trakon was the first human to ever ride a dragon," the stone man confirmed.

The rock man once more touched the water, and Daxon watched the fight between Trakon and Jessa, her jealousy of his friendship with Rakisa apparent. Dax saw her storm off, alone once more, never to look back.

The pool rippled, and Dax saw Jessa huddled beneath a large boulder, tears once more streaming down her face. Almost absently, she reached up and caught one, the perfectly round droplet balancing on the tip of her finger.

"Why must I be alone?" she whispered, staring intently at her reddish-hued tear as if she had never seen anything like it before.

The tear began to tremble, and ever so slowly, it rose from her finger to suspend in the air above her hand. She beheld it, mesmerized, as it gradually began to spin. It picked up momentum quickly, and soon began to expand until it was the size of a pebble, then an egg, and, finally, the size of a man's fist. *Perfectly circular*, Dax thought as he watched the reddish hue clear until he could clearly make out a single dragon egg within the newly-formed Orb. The sphere began to float away from Jessa, who quickly jumped up and followed it.

~Ripple~

The sphere was now floating above the dragon egg in the vision. Jessa stared, transfixed, then tentatively reached out a hand to touch the shell, which was yellow with jagged, green stripes. Almost immediately, the egg began to move, causing her to jump back, startled. Soon cracks appeared in the smooth surface of the egg, and a small, clawed foot emerged, followed by a tiny, yellow dragon's head.

The hatchling was much smaller than Drakthira had been, no longer than a man's arm from its snout to the tip of its tail. It wobbled over to Jessa and wrapped its body around her legs, crying for food. She scooped it up in her arms, cooing at it and rubbing it along its eye ridges. She took what Dax assumed was a piece of meat from a previous meal out of a small pack she carried on her back and fed it to the little dragon.

~Ripple~

Now the hatchling was almost a year old by Daxon's estimation and close to the time it would normally leave its mother. He saw Jessa, still with the orb floating close by her, as she tried to feed the young dragon pieces of meat from a stag she had brought down. The dragon, however, was refusing to eat the meat provided for it. It wanted to hunt for itself. Spreading its wings, the dragon took to the sky, but only managed to get a short distance away before Jessa cried out.

Daxon watched as a thin, red line shot from the orb, attaching itself to the dragon, forming a tether to hinder the dragon's ability to fly away. The dragon crashed to the ground instead, roaring in anger. It regained its feet, advancing on Jessa, its fury easily recognizable by its flaming eyes.

Jessa backed away from the beast, now much larger than she, her hands held out before her. She was speaking in a soothing voice, although Dax couldn't quite make out the words. The dragon didn't slow, growling deep within its chest, and flames began to erupt from its mouth around its snout.

Just as Dax thought the beast would blast Jessa with fire, she pointed at it again and said, "You will obey me!"

Glancing at the pool above, Dax watched as the orb began to glow with magical energy. A fine net of energy emerged from the sphere, engulfing the young dragon. The more the dragon tried to escape the energy net, the deeper the energy was absorbed into its scales.

Eventually, the dragon quieted. Jessa approached it once more, laying her hand on its snout and stroking the beast lovingly. She picked up the piece of meat she had tried to feed it previously and held it out again. This time the dragon took the proffered meat placidly, devouring the entire stag in this way. When it was finished eating, Jessa stroked it again, whispering "good girl" over and over.

~Ripple~

Jessa was standing beside a waterfall and the yellow dragon was once more trying to escape. Dax surmised that not much time had passed; for the dragon was only slightly larger than it had been in the previous scene. Dragons grew their entire lives, but the first year they almost doubled in size every few months. After that, their growth slowed tremendously, by only a few feet each year. If this dragon were older, it was by only a mere week or so in Daxon's estimation.

He watched as Jessa once more brought the young dragon out of the sky, angering it again. She was crying, screaming at the beast at the top of her lungs, "Why can't you just be with me?! Why do you keep trying to leave?!"

Unlike the last time, the dragon didn't attempt to confront Jessa. Instead, it kept launching itself into the sky, hoping it would be able to put enough distance between itself and the orb to get away, but again to no avail. Each time the orb brought it down again, until the beast lay, exhausted, upon the ground.

Eventually, Jessa stopped crying, and Dax heard her say to herself, "I need to find a way to make it love me so it will want to stay with me."

~Ripple~

When the image cleared this time, Daxon was certain that at least a year or more had passed. The dragon was noticeably larger, but what caught his attention was the dragon's drastic change in appearance. The great beast's scales had lost their previous luster and looked dull and unkempt, and its eyes had lost their fire. He wondered if it were now blind, and looked in the pool above once more, and gasped at what he saw.

Red, magical webbing surrounded the dragon's wings, preventing it from spreading them and keeping them folded in close to its body. It trudged along behind Jessa and her floating orb, occasionally stumbling, but always managing to catch itself before falling down completely. Each time it stumbled, Jessa would speak softly to it, encouraging it ever onward.

~*Ripple*~

Jessa and the yellow dragon were now sitting in the shadow of the godling's ancient tree. It looked to Dax like the dragon was almost dead. Its head was lying in Jessa's lap, and she was crying over it and stroking it, whispering softly. He felt immense pity for the poor creature, never having been able to live its own life, but always enslaved for as long as it could remember. He could tell the dragon had lost all interest in living and was simply waiting to die. No more than a few years old, it had already decided death was preferable to its current existence.

Jessa wailed, clearly distraught. She screamed to the sky, "Please! Please save her! I love her!"

Although he didn't condone anything he had seen Jessa do thus far, Daxon couldn't help but feel sorry for the woman. She was clearly lonely, and in desperate need of a friend. That she loved the dragon he did not doubt, but what she didn't see was that her possessive love was killing its very will to live.

The godling, too, must have heard her cries within his great tree. Dax watched as Aarlian emerged, his little stick man golem by his side, and approach the crying woman. He took in the dying dragon, then spoke to Jessa.

"You must let her go, Jessa," Dax heard him say.

68

Surprised, Jessa asked, "H-How do you know my name?"

"I know many things. Like I know this dragon is dying, and wishes it so. You cannot save what doesn't want to be saved."

"Can you?" she asked him, pleading with her eyes. "Please, I will do anything to save her. Anything at all, just tell me you can save her," she sobbed imploringly.

"Why do you wish to save her so badly?" the godling asked her.

Jessa looked down at the dragon's head, still stroking it gently, and whispered, "She's my only friend here. Without her I'm all alone."

Aarlian regarded the woman for a long moment. Finally, he said, "There is a way to save the dragon. But," he said, raising his index finger to keep her from speaking out, "it will not be easy. I can keep the dragon alive for two days. Much of its magic has already left it, and will need to be replenished. To do this, you must bring back some of the Myste."

"The mist?" she asked, not understanding.

"You will not find it here, you must travel to the borders of Darkenfel, and on to the edge of the world. There, you will find the abyss, and you must capture some of it and bring it back here."

"But... how do I capture fog?" Jessa questioned.

"The orb you have should work just fine. It has more than enough magic to contain the Myste," Aarlian answered her.

Jessa glanced at the orb she had somehow made from her tear. She hadn't given much thought about the magical properties of it; she simply knew it gave her what she wanted. At least, most of the time.

"What will the Myste do? How will it save my dragon?" she asked.

"If you manage to capture some and bring it back here, I will use it to replace some of the magic lost from this dragon. You see, the Myste protects Darkenfel's borders, preventing intruders from entering, and residents from leaving. It consists mostly of dragon magic, which is closely attuned to their souls. So, you see, as the magic leaves this dragon, so does its soul. To save it, we will need to replace it. But, even then, I can't guarantee it will work. This dragon has no will to live. You have tried to force it to bend to your will because you fear being alone. That is not friendship. That is enslavement. If you want to truly bond with this beast, you must do so on its terms. Friendship, true friendship, cannot be forced," the godling finished.

Jessa hung her head in shame and Dax watched as a single, reddish hued tear perched on the tip of her nose and hung there, suspended. "I understand," she whispered.

Jessa rose, and with a final pat on the yellow dragon's head, she turned and said to Aarlian, "I will return before two days' time with what you require. Please, keep her alive until then."

Aarlian nodded as Jessa took the orb in her hand and said, "Take me to the Myste."

In a flash of red, she was gone.

~*Ripple*~

Now Dax saw Jessa standing at the edge of the Myste. She looked tired, but determined. She approached the abyss, hesitantly, somehow sensing its power, even though she had never encountered it before. She walked a short distance inside the Myste, far enough to be surrounded by the dangerous, grey fog, but still close enough to the edge to easily find her way out again.

She spoke some words to the orb, but Dax wasn't close enough to hear. He turned to the stone man. "Can we get closer?" he asked.

"No," the stone man answered. "In the realm of the Myste, I am not master."

Daxon filed that information away for later. He found it interesting that even the earth could not penetrate the Myste's magic.

He turned back to the pool, seeing the orb collect the Myste by simply forming an opening and closing around it. Once Jessa felt there was plenty swirling around inside of the strange globe, she crossed the boundary out of the abyss, the orb grasped tightly in her hand.

~Ripple~

Jessa stood once more before the ancient godling tree. Her hair was tangled and dirt streaked her face and clothes. Dax wasn't sure how she had traversed Darkenfel, but he guessed the orb wasn't able to take her directly to the Myste. Perhaps like the stone man, the orb was limited in its interactions with other magic. The woman looked almost nothing like the Jessa he had seen before. She had bags under her eyes, a clear sign she hadn't slept in the time she had been gone, and her shoulders sagged tiredly.

She held the globe out to Aarlian, who merely shook his head sadly. "I thought I could keep her alive for at least two days, but she rejected my magic. She didn't want to live any longer," he said. "She passed just a few minutes before your arrival."

Jessa merely stood there, trembling, her shoulders heaving. Dax thought she must be crying, but her long, dirty hair was covering her face and he couldn't be sure.

He heard her, then, her voice thick and gravelly, as if she hadn't had anything to drink in quite a while. Her sobs wracked her body. She clutched at her midsection, hugging herself as she rocked back and forth on the heels of her feet.

"What am I supposed to do now?" she asked no one in particular, her eyes wild as she looked upon the body of the yellow dragon.

Suddenly, her eyes snapped to Aarlian. Pointing her finger at him, her voice unexpectedly loud, she said, "Fix her. Bring her back."

"I'm afraid I cannot," he said, turning back towards his tree.

Jessa watched him and his stick man golem retreat back to the massive tree they called home. She watched, motionless, as Aarlian disappeared back into his tree, seeming to meld seamlessly into its massive trunk, the little stick man a few yards behind.

Without warning, Jessa rushed forward just as the stick man reached the tree and grasped the little golem around its twiggy neck. Dax saw the stick man start to struggle, trying to free itself from her grasp. When that didn't work, he simply began to merge with the tree, becoming an unassuming branch within seconds.

Still angry, Jessa yanked at the newly formed branch, finally managing to split it away from the trunk just as the tree began to disappear. Dax saw thick, red sap begin to bleed from where she had split the branch. With a final wrench, she freed the branch from the tree just as it disappeared completely.

In the pool above, Daxon saw the branch glowing a brilliant green, evidence of the life magic living within it. Where it had separated from the trunk of the tree, streamers of thick, bloody sap oozed out, and where it hit the ground, flowers sprang to life.

"*BRING HER BACK!*" Jessa shouted, pointing the staff at the lifeless body of the dragon.

Immediately the orb rushed to the broken limb, embedding itself in a space near the top where the limb forked. Dax could see the red lightning storm of magic from the orb join with the Myste magic it had trapped inside itself, and the life magic from the severed limb. They swirled around each other, finally merging into one, and shot from the orb into the body of the dragon.

Daxon watched as the body of the dragon began to glow from the inside. The magic seemed to saturate every particle of its being. Eventually, it made its way out, and he saw the dragon's scales regain their lustrous, shiny color. The magic traveled from the dragon's tail, transforming everything it touched, renewing it, until it finally ended at the snout and stopped.

For a few long moments, nothing happened. Then, Dax saw the dragon's sides rise and fall as it took a breath, and soon after, it blinked open its eyes. The beast seemed confused, but when it saw Jessa, a horrendous roar escaped from its maw.

Lurching to her feet, the yellow dragon advanced on Jessa, fury in her eyes. Dax could see her taking deep breaths, a sure sign she was stoking the fire in her belly.

"Why do you hate me?" Jessa wailed at it while backing away. "I brought you back! I gave you life again!"

Unmoved, the dragon continued her advance.

"Why can't you love me? I have done everything for you!" Jessa pleaded, tears streaming down her face.

Dax saw the yellow dragon take a deep breath, preparing to roast Jessa where she stood. Flames licked out of her maw and around her teeth. Jessa also saw the flames, and understood what it meant. Just as the dragon drew back its head to exhale the deadly fire, she shouted, "STOP! YOU WILL OBEY ME, EVEN IF YOU DON'T LOVE ME!"

Magic once more shot forth from the Orb, now embedded in the godling staff. Dax saw it enter the dragon's body, and when it emerged, he couldn't help but gasp aloud.

Twisting at the end of the beam of magic was a luminescent light so bright it hurt to look upon it. It was shaped like the dragon from which it had come, but smaller, and ephemeral. Tiny, thin membranes seemed to attach the shimmering light within the dragon's body, but as he watched, the magic from the staff severed a piece of the substance, drawing it back with it into the Orb. Once it vanished into the globe, the remainder snapped back into the dragon's body, and the yellow dragon roared in agony, writhing upon the ground.

Not wanting to witness the poor creature's misery, Dax looked at the Orb and saw it was swirling with a brilliant yellow color. A color so rich it made every other shade of yellow pale in comparison, and could only be called a "…True color," he whispered.

Not wanting to see any more, but knowing he needed to gain as much knowledge as he could, Dax watched as Jessa approached the now quiet yellow dragon. When she was just a few feet away from it, she said, "Rise."

Obediently, the dragon rose to her feet, looking at Jessa for her next command.

Jessa climbed atop the dragon's back, raised her staff in the air and said, "Let's go."

As the vision of Jessa riding the yellow dragon over Darkenfel faded, Dax once more felt his world spinning out of control. He shut his eyes against the dizziness, wishing what he had just witnessed had been nothing more than a dream, but all the while knowing it was not.

Chapter Six

Every new beginning comes from some other beginning's end.

~ Seneca

As Dax readjusted to his surroundings, he noticed that Trakon was looking at him expectantly, waiting to hear what he had discovered.

"I know how the Orb was made, as well as how Jessa got the staff," he said. He then told them what he had seen, sharing the visions with Drakthira as he did so. When he reached the end of the tale, Trakon lowered his head in sadness while Drakthira growled deep in her chest.

"Is there a way we can get a staff from you as well, Aarlian?" Dax asked.

Before the godling could answer, Trakon shook his head. "It won't do any good, Dax," he began. "The staff is a part of the spell, that's true, but even if we are able to get another, we would still be missing a vital piece of the puzzle."

"What do you mean? What piece? We already know where the Orb is." Dax said.

"So far it looks like Jessa used at least three different sources of magic to create the Orb." He held up one finger. "First, she used the Blood of the Mountain within her to create the Orb." Holding up another finger, he continued, "Second, she used the Myste, which she captured and held within the Orb." He held up a final finger. "And third, she used the life magic within the staff."

Dax continued to look at him blankly. "And…?"

"And then there are the intangibles. Why did she cast the spell? Was it out of love? Out of fear? Or simply because she was lonely, or maybe a combination of all? You see, intangibles are just as important as the actual components of the spell if you want to undo it. Unless, of course, you can find a source of power greater than the spell itself and simply rip it apart," he explained.

"So you are saying that unless we can find a power greater than that used to create the spell, we first have to know the reasoning behind the spell?" Dax asked incredulously.

"Yes, that's exactly right. Not only that, but even if we take possession of the Orb, that alone will not guarantee that we also possess the Blood of the Mountain. I suspect we would need our own supply of that as well," the old man continued.

Sensing Daxon's frustration, Drakthira cut in and asked, *In a perfect world, wizard, what would be the easiest and safest way to destroy the Orb and free the dragons?*

Trakon didn't answer at first, simply gazed off, staring at nothing. Finally, he said, "The easiest way to break the spell is to have the one who originally cast the spell to undo it."

"You mean Jessa?" Dax asked, his voice rising in frustration. "We don't even know if she is still alive! According to the history of Goldspine, Jessa lived over six hundred years ago." He ran his hand through his hair, careful not to prick himself with the quills lying beneath it. He paced back and forth, and then suddenly stopped.

"Wait," Dax said, looking at Trakon pointedly. "You told me you are over six hundred years old, and I believe you. That means you were here on Darkenfel when Daegonlot was separated from the mainland. Why did you never tell us how it happened?"

"I have given a lot of thought to that as well, Dax. The truth is, I don't remember Daegonlot separating from the mainland, and I can only guess it happened during the time Jessa and I were still together, before I met Rakisa. We made our home in the far northern part of Darkenfel. There were no other people around that area, and we both preferred it that way. At one time we had come across a small village of humans, probably a week's travel to the southeast, and they told us of constant raids between themselves and another village a day's travel to the west. We wanted no part of that, having come from a more civilized world, so we moved on. I didn't realize Daegonlot had separated until years afterwards, when I was flying with Rakisa. It was one of the last flights we ever took together."

Aarlian spoke up, "It wouldn't have mattered if he were there, Daxon. No one, not those who were there or those who were not, remember how Daegonlot was separated from Darkenfel. Only the earth truly remembers."

"Why?" Dax asked, genuinely curious.

"We like to call it a natural defense, but the truth is Darkenfel is the apex of many timelines. This has its repercussions. Currents overlap each other, and ripples of significant events sometimes have an effect on other timelines. History becomes fluid. Do we remember what truly happened or was it simply an event from another timeline that bled over into Darkenfel? Then you have places on Darkenfel like the Myste, a step away from the currents of time.

"What I'm trying to say is that Darkenfel doesn't adhere to any standard of time like other worlds. There is simply too much magic, and too many crossing timelines to make it so. For that reason, residents of Darkenfel simply stop trying to remember specifics even though they think they remember. Just like the history you were taught on Goldspine, Daxon. The only thing really agreed upon is that it happened in the race wars, the rest is simply conjecture. It's the same everywhere."

"But, I have aged since I have come here," Trakon interjected. "If time doesn't really exist here, how did that happen?"

"I'm not saying time doesn't exist here, I'm simply saying there is no true standard of measurement. You told Dax you were over six hundred years old, but by what measurement? The world's you came from? How do you know that even applies here?" the godling asked.

Trakon considered the godling's words. It made sense when he thought about it. Even the geography of Darkenfel changed sporadically; portals would form out of nowhere and close just as quickly. Why would time be any easier to track?

"Sylas still needs to ask his question. After that, if you really think Jessa may still be alive, we will try to track her down and see if we can convince her to reverse what she's done," Dax said to Trakon. "Even if we can't convince her to help, we may be able to get the staff away from her, or find out more about how to undo the spell."

Trakon nodded absently, his mind preoccupied with his thoughts.

Aarlian looked at Sylas. "Are you ready?"

Sylas barked in response.

Sylas watched Aarlian. He knew from seeing the others ask their questions he would need to wait until Aarlian's eyes began to look different. Then the man-beast-that-smelled-like-a-plant would ask him something. He also knew his answer would determine if the godling would grant Trakon's request to make him like Dax; entirely free from the Myste. But, he didn't think about that. Here in this place he didn't feel the pull of the Myste, and if he had to return, he would put it off for as long as he was able to help his friends.

The godling's eyes opened, blazing white. He asked, "SYLAS, CREATURE OF MYSTE AND MAGIC, IF I COULD GRANT YOU BUT ONE WISH, WHAT WOULD IT BE?"

Unlike the others, Sylas didn't have to think of his answer. He showed the godling a memory of Dax chasing him around their campsite, trying to recover the bedroll he had taken. Dax was laughing. It was a good memory. Once it faded away, another took its place, this time of him and Drakthira sleeping peacefully together, side by side, after sharing a stag he had brought down for their food. She looked content and full. It was a good memory.

Finally, he showed the godling his favorite memory of all. The memory of Trakon inadvertently changing him with his life magic, the first time he had been able to feel anything other than hunger. That memory faded, and immediately one of Trakon playing with him, throwing a ball, took its place. He hadn't realized at first that Trakon wanted him to go get it, and the old man had laughed until his belly hurt at the quizzical expressions on Sylas' face as he tried to teach him to fetch. It, too, was a good memory.

Lastly, Sylas showed a vision of Trakon, staring off into the distance, murmuring to himself. His eyes were full of sadness, and only one sentence came clearly to Sylas; "I'm sorry I let you down, Rakisa."

Sylas didn't know how to free the dragons, but he did understand Jessa had done something terrible to them, and especially to Rakisa. He also knew he never wanted the terrible something to happen to his dragon friend, 'Thira. More than anything, he wanted to erase the sadness he saw in Trakon's eyes and protect his dragon friend from any harm.

The godling took in all of Sylas' memories, understanding the jumble of visions as clearly as if the dog had spoken to him. He said, "SYLAS, YOU ARE INDEED WORTHY OF THE GIFT TRAKON HAS BESTOWED UPON YOU. I, TOO, WILL GRANT YOU MY GIFT AND FREE YOU FROM HAVING TO RETURN TO THE MYSTE. DRINK AND YOU WILL BE FILLED WITH MY EARTHEN MAGIC, AND YOU, TOO MAY SHARE MY KNOWLEDGE."

Sylas approached the opened rock and lapped up all the remaining liquid. He felt it travel through him, a not unpleasant feeling of warmth traversing throughout his body. He felt like every cell within him was bursting with life and energy, and his body shook in response.

"NOW, COME WITH ME," said the being within the godling.

Sylas saw the entity depart from Aarlian's body. It became ephemeral, sparkling in the sun, and Sylas quickly changed to his mist form and followed it.

Sylas followed the sparkling green energy down a dark tunnel. The tunnel stretched out for miles, twisting and turning in the darkness. After they had gone many miles and sped through crevices no person would ever be able to squeeze through, they finally emerged into a large, underground cavern. Sylas reformed into his solid state and after a moment, the glowing green energy sank into the floor beside him.

The giant dog looked around. Gems of all kinds and of all sizes were embedded in the walls and ceiling of the cavern. He saw diamonds the size of a man, and rubies larger than he was, yet, being a dog, these things held no value for him.

The floor beside him began to tremble slightly, and soon after a hand emerged as if the floor was made of liquid instead of solid stone. Sylas cocked his head quizzically as he watched the stone man emerge from the cavern floor, gems embedded all over his body. He noticed in this form, the stone man did not smell like a plant, but instead like a mixture of things; rock, dirt, grass, and even a little like running water and blood.

"Greetings, Sylas," said the stone man. "What would you like to ask of me?"

Unlike with the others, the stone man did not make any suggestions. That was fine with Sylas since he already knew what he wanted to ask. He focused on the name of the one Trakon wanted to find: Jessa. Where was she now?

The stone man's eyes began to glow dimly. He moved to stand beside a large, clear diamond embedded in the wall. With a gesture the gem blazed to life, glowing so brilliantly Sylas averted his eyes. When it dimmed, he saw Jessa standing in a cavern much like the one he stood within now but without the gems.

He moved closer to the image. Something seemed wrong. He had the sense he was seeing Jessa as she was now, at this moment, yet, she wasn't moving, merely standing still. He sniffed at the image, surprised when her scent came through clearly to his keen nose. She smelled like lavender overlaid with the coppery scent of blood. But not ordinary blood. Something about it was different. Earthy. More than anything, she smelled like fear.

Focusing as much as he was able, Sylas could just make out the faint reddish glow surrounding the woman in the image, as if she were somehow caught in a thin globe of magical energy. Her eyes were wide as she stared at something Sylas couldn't see. The rise and fall of her chest gave away the fact she was still alive, but she seemed to be trapped. And afraid.

Sylas took a last, long sniff at the image and the woman trapped within, and filed it away in his memory. He would track her down for Trakon. Then she could release the dragons and everyone would be happy. And he would have another dragon friend to play with and share meals with. The thought made his stub tail wag for just a moment as the image in the diamond faded away.

The stone man turned to him. "Sylas, there is something you must know before we return to your friends," he began. "I didn't want to tell you this in front of everyone, but you must know." He stopped and took a deep breath.

Sylas wasn't sure what the stone man wanted to tell him, but he understood enough of body language to understand it would not be good news.

"The life magic which Trakon infused into you is the sustaining force for the Myste which is in you. The magic I gave you will reinforce your earth magic temporarily, but eventually the Myste within you will prove overpowering, and you will revert to the original Myste's creation." He looked sad as he said it, or at least as sad as a man made of stone could manage. "I have no power over the Myste. In its own way, the Myste is probably the most powerful magic on Daegonlot. It consumes all other types of magic, absorbing it, merging with it to create, consume, or destroy. I wish there was something I could do, but I thought you should know."

Sylas knew the stone man was telling him the truth; he could smell if the creature was lying. It made him sad to think he might revert back to his former self and become a danger to his

84

friends. He cocked his head questioningly at the stone man as if to say *how much time do I have?*

"I don't know how long you have," the stone man answered the unspoken question. "It seems it has been feeding for a long time, but it's possible, even likely, it will go faster the longer you are away from the Myste. You will no longer feel the pull, but the Myste within you is devouring your earth magic to maintain itself, and I fear it will only get worse the longer you stay away."

Sylas dipped his head in acknowledgement. He changed to his mist form and, with the stone man, glided back to the ever sunny Grove.

Trakon and Daxon were talking quietly with Drakthira when they saw Sylas' misty, grey form enter the clearing along with the glistening, green energy. Sylas reformed beside Trakon and watched with his friends as the green substance entered Aarlian, who opened his eyes a few moments later.

"I hope you found the knowledge you were seeking, Sylas," Aarlian said. The godling looked diminished somehow, as if the strain of communicating with the Earth had taken a large toll on him. He stood and said to the group, "Please rest. You will be safe for tonight." He murmured something under his breath and clapped his hands together, and immediately the sun was replaced with the moon, and darkness reigned in The Grove. Then he was gone.

85

Dax looked at Sylas, wishing he could communicate with the big dog and find out what he had learned. Trakon asked, "What do we do now?"

Dax began to answer, but suddenly felt very tired. "I don't know, yet," he managed to say. The ground had never felt so soft. "We will figure it out in the morning."

Trakon, too, felt his eyelids closing. He tried to protest, but eventually just nodded in agreement, stretching out upon the ground. Within minutes he was snoring loudly.

Drakthira and Sylas exchanged amused looks, then the big dog curled up by her side and he, too, began to snore. 'Thira could feel the magic emanating from the tree and knew it was responsible for the sudden sleepiness overcoming the rest of the party. She could feel it as well, but it had no real hold over her, and she knew she could easily shake it off. Instead, not knowing what tomorrow would bring or when they would have another full night's rest, she allowed the magic to overcome her senses and drifted off into darkness.

Chapter Seven

The fiercest serpent may be overcome by a swarm of ants.

~ Isoroku Yamamoto

When Dax awoke the next morning he found himself back in their original camp. There was no sign of The Grove or the godling. He inched himself out from beneath Drakthira's wing where he had been sleeping. He couldn't remember the last time he had slept so well, and wondered to himself if that had to do more with the Grove, or the warmth of 'Thira's scales. But in any case, he felt refreshed and ready to take on anything. Taking in these familiar surroundings, Dax found Trakon sleeping on his bedroll that was pushed up against Sylas' back. The old man had his arm thrown over the dog and both were snoring loudly.

He chuckled quietly at the scene and heard Drakthira do the same. Glad she was awake, he leaned up against her large, scaly chest and laid his head against her cheek. *Where should we go from here, 'Thira?* he asked.

She nuzzled him, then raised her head to look at the old man and the dog once more. She didn't know how to answer Daxon. The quest before them seemed vast and she was unsure what their next steps should be. Up to this point it seemed they had always known what their next move should be, but in light of all they had recently learned, she was as puzzled as Dax. Should they try to rejoin Daegonlot to Darkenfel? Or should they try to find Jessa? Maybe instead of either of those options, they should seek out a great power that could do both. She simply didn't know.

At that moment, Trakon let out a snore so loud it awoke Sylas, who, alarmed, immediately dissipated. The old man, who had been leaning against the dog as he slept, fell over and his arm that had been draped over Sylas hit the ground, jarring him awake. Dax and 'Thira shared another chuckle as the old man rubbed the sleep from his eyes and sat up. Sylas, realizing there was no immediate threat, reformed atop Trakon and began to lick his face to help him wake up. Trakon sputtered and tried to push him off, but it was like pushing a boulder and finally he tried to hide his face by pushing it into the dog's chest. Sylas, unperturbed, continued to lick the old man's head, making his wisps of hair stand up in comical angles.

"Let him up, Sylas, I'm hungry, and Trakon cooks the best eggs," Dax said, laughing aloud. Reluctantly, Sylas removed himself and Trakon got to work preparing breakfast for himself and Dax.

Once breakfast was over, Dax approached Trakon to get his opinion on how to proceed. Before he could even broach the subject, however, Sylas materialized directly in front of him and barked loudly. Daxon regarded the dog a moment, then tried to step around him and continue on his way, but once more, Sylas blocked his path. Instead of barking, the giant dog took the elf's arm gently in his mouth and began pulling him along.

"Where are you taking me, Sylas?" Daxon asked.

Sylas released his arm and simply looked at him, head cocked to the side. Then he looked off to the west and whined loudly.

Sylas wants us to follow him, Drakthira supplied helpfully.

Trakon walked up and stood by Daxon's side and together they looked off to the west, following Sylas' gaze. "What lies that way?" Dax asked the old man.

"A few scattered human villages if memory serves me right," Trakon began. "It's hard to say now, I haven't been that way in a long time. Most of the villages were wiped out and few humans remained the last time I passed through. Beyond that is the Salt Crystal Lake, and after that, the Crimson Peak Mountains."

"Why is it called Salt Crystal Lake?" Dax asked. He had grown up on Daegonlot, and before that, lived within the Myste. Darkenfel was still a mostly unexplored mystery to him.

"Hopefully you won't have to find out why," the old man said ominously. "It's surrounded by desert and quicksand. The lake itself is so full of salt it's poisonous to drink."

"Sounds wonderful," Dax said wryly, looking at Sylas intently.

His mind made up, Dax nodded at the big dog and stroked the silvery grey fur on his neck. "You have never let us down before, boy. If you think we need to go west, we will follow you."

Solemnly, Sylas turned and began trotting westward. After just a few moments, he became ephemeral and soared swiftly towards his destination. Trakon mounted Drakthira, and with a powerful leap, they were airborn, with Dax gliding along beside them.

During the following two days, Dax wished numerous times that he knew their final destination, so that he could teleport the travelers and shorten this part of the journey. He had been able to scout ahead for the godling simply because he grew up on Daegonlot and knew every inch of the relatively small island. He knew nothing of Darkenfel, had never even flown over this part of it, much less walked it.

The sun beat down on them from overhead, seemingly more intense the farther west they went. Sweat trickled down from his hairline into his eyes, making them sting. Cursing, he wiped his forehead. The party stopped in the shade of a small copse of trees to rest and eat from their dwindling food supplies, but even in the shade it was abysmally hot.

Dax finished off the last bite of some dried jerky and stared off to the west. According to Trakon's estimation they would reach the Salt Crystal Lake by day's end. They would be skirting the southern edge of the lake, which would still take about a day if the old dragonrider's memory was correct. This would be a day of danger, traversing some of the most treacherous ground in Darkenfel, full of quicksand pits and desert, completely devoid of any water other than the lake itself, which was full of salt and other minerals.

Dax turned and looked at the other members of the party. Trakon was sweating heavily and drinking deeply from his water cask. Even Sylas seemed affected by the heat, panting heavily where he lay. Only Drakthira seemed unaffected, possibly because her scales reflected most of the heat away from her body. Daxon was thankful for that. He hated seeing 'Thira experience discomfort, and there was no way Trakon would have been able to travel on foot over the distance they had to cover if she couldn't carry him.

Can you smell any water close by, 'Thira? he asked his dragon companion.

He saw her out of the corner of his eye stretch out her long neck and sniff deeply. *Yes,* she answered, *there is a river or stream a few hours ahead.*

Daxon was grateful for their good fortune. Most of the land he had seen on Darkenfel was lush and water was not hard to come by, therefore, they hadn't bothered packing more than just a few casks. He figured if they could get across the desert within a day they would be fine with what they could carry as long as they drank as much as they could from the stream before setting out. 'Thira shouldn't need any additional water at all, and Dax thought he and Sylas would probably be alright if they drank sparingly. It was mostly Trakon he was worried about. He would need to drink regularly to stay hydrated, especially with as much as he was sweating.

"Alright, let's go," he said. "Drakthira says there is water a few hours ahead. We will camp by the source tonight and drink our fill before starting out tomorrow."

He *dimmed* his body, floating into the air where he hovered while Trakon mounted Drakthira. Once again, they continued westward.

As promised, a few hours before dusk the band of travelers came upon a small stream fed from an underground spring. Although he knew they could reach the desert outskirts if they kept going, Dax called for a halt and made camp.

"Drink as much and as often as you can tonight without making yourselves sick," he said. "Tomorrow we will enter the desert and will need to conserve as much water as we can."

There was little shade to be found even this close to water. Dax walked along the streambed a short distance until he found a curve where the stream widened and created a small pool of slow moving water. He removed his clothing and entered the pool to cool his heated body.

There is a pool down this way, 'Thira. Tell Trakon to follow my tracks. The water feels great and he can wash off the dirt and sweat.

He allowed himself a few more minutes to revel in the coolness of the water, washing the sweat and grime from his body, before stepping out and getting dressed. Just as he finished pulling on his boots, Trakon arrived, his eyes lighting up as he looked longingly at the small pool.

"It's all yours," Dax said. "I need to scout around, see if I can find some fresh meat to bolster our supplies."

The old man nodded and began undressing as Dax walked off, still following the streambed away from their camp. He scoured the ground, looking for any signs of game. Shortly, he came across some hoof prints in the soft mud alongside the streambed and began following them. He walked quietly, hoping he could catch his prey unaware, and was rewarded for his efforts when he spotted a small, deer-like creature cropping the sparse grass beside the streambed. He felled it instantly, stealing its life force before it even knew he was there.

He slung the carcass over his shoulder, feeling rejuvenated with the creature's life energy coursing through him, and teleported back to their campsite. He dressed the deer and started it roasting on a makeshift spit he carved from a branch he found lying on the ground nearby.

Turning from the cooking meat, he saw 'Thira dozing but saw no sign of Sylas. *Probably hunting*, he thought.

As if on cue, Sylas appeared carrying a large carcass of an animal Dax had never seen before. It resembled a huge rat, but was hairless and had no eyes. He settled down with 'Thira and they began to eat.

The meat Dax was roasting was done so he moved it away from the fire. He was beginning to get worried about Trakon and wondered if the old man had fallen asleep in the pool. Just as he was about to teleport back to the pool to check on him, Trakon walked into camp looking much better than he had before.

"Thank you for showing me the pool, Dax, it was very refreshing. And for finding some fresh meat for supper," he added, seeing the roasted meat.

Dax nodded, and they both settled down to eat. Watching the old man out of the corner of his eye, Dax sensed there was something bothering him. He was staring vacantly toward the west, unease apparent on his face. "What is it, Trakon?" he asked.

The old man looked at Dax and smiled briefly. "Nothing, really," he began. "It's just I can't feel any life energy coming from the west. It's as if there is a giant black hole in the earth devoid of life of any kind. It makes me uneasy to think I will not be able to use my magic is all."

Dax followed the old man's gaze, now a little uneasy himself. He remembered taking Trakon into the Myste, and the strange way the magic within had affected him. He had unwittingly called forth a dragon from his mind. Be that as it may, he would feel better if Trakon were able to use his magic if needed. They had faced enough perils to know he couldn't count on always being around when the old man needed help.

"Maybe it's just shielded," Dax supplied helpfully.

Trakon's brow creased further. So quietly Dax almost missed it, he muttered, "I'm not sure that would be better."

Mid-morning the next day the small party was once again airborne above the shimmering white desert sand. Dax had never seen sand so white. Heat rose from the ground and distorted the air. The wind didn't stir; not even a breeze disturbed the white blanket. Drakthira labored to keep aloft in the absence of any thermals to help. Dax knew she wouldn't be able to fly much longer, especially with the added weight of Trakon.

By noon the glistening water of the lake was in view and Dax signaled for the party to land. There was no shade to provide a refuge as far as the eye could see, so under the full brunt of the midday sun they rested, drenched in sweat and miserable.

Not really hungry, but knowing he needed to eat to maintain his strength, Dax wolfed down his ration of food, a strip of jerky and some dried kalacas fruit. He took a small sip out of one of the casks of water they had filled at the stream the day before and stood up.

"I'm going to scout ahead," he said. "It's getting difficult for Drakthira to keep flying without any wind to help bolster flight. She needs to rest." He looked at Trakon. "You and Sylas stay and watch over her. I will teleport back and get you all once I find a good place to camp tonight."

Trakon nodded wearily. He wanted to argue about Dax going off by himself, but of them all, Dax was the best equipped for a solitary foray.

Daxon *dimmed* and disappeared. Once he was gone, Trakon walked to the edge of the water. On the surface it looked so serene. He picked up a palm sized rock and threw it into the water. The rock landed with a loud *slap*, then slowly began to sink below the surface. He walked along the shore, careful not to touch any of the foul water. Bones from various creatures littered the shore, bleached white by the sun so they blended in well with the sand surrounding them.

He walked back to where Drakthira was napping, Sylas curled up in her shadow, also dozing. He joined the big dog, grateful to get out of the sun. It felt at least ten degrees cooler in the shade. He reached out with his magic, trying to sense any sort of life within this desolate wasteland. He wasn't expecting to find anything and was mildly surprised to find a tiny bit of life beneath the sand. He focused on it, trying to determine what it was. It felt small, yet large at the same time. He shifted his position to get more comfortable, and immediately felt the things in the sand surge toward him. The sudden movement felt... hungry. He froze. Once he quit moving they stopped, milling about in a confusing mass.

A cold trickle of fear swept down his spine. The things in the sand were, themselves, quite small, no larger than an ant, yet felt large due to the sheer number of them. He moved his foot slightly, testing to see if he was correct and they were drawn to movement, and felt them once more surge toward him, then stop. Waiting.

A drop of sweat dripped down from his forehead into his eyes, making them sting, but he didn't dare move to wipe it away. Panic threatened to overwhelm him, but he pushed it down, trying to think of what to do. He looked at the huge dog curled up beside him, silently hoping he wouldn't wake up at that moment and attract the creatures in the sand.

Trakon looked around quickly, hoping he had missed something, a rock or boulder jutting up from the ground, but there was nothing. Just then, 'Thira's tail twitched and he once more felt the lifeforms surge toward the movement. This time when they stopped, they were only a few feet below the ground and maybe eight feet away. He would have to think of something quick.

96

He carefully laid a hand on Sylas. "Sylas, wake up. Mist form, don't touch the ground!" he said, nearly shouting as he felt the dog's movement under his hand. The dog quickly dissipated and Trakon caught his hand before it could thump to the ground.

"Wake Drakthira, Sylas. We have to get off of the ground," he instructed.

He didn't look behind him to see if Sylas was doing as he asked. Instead he focused on the beings in the sand. So far they hadn't moved any closer. He heard 'Thira yawn behind and growl grumpily, the rumbling sending small tremors through the sand which he felt where he sat. The tiny organisms surged once more.

Throwing caution to the wind, Trakon jumped to his feet and yelled, "Off the sand! Hurry!"

He ran to the dragon that was still lying on the ground, looking at him as if he had lost his mind. He leaped onto her back, feeling the creatures reach the surface of the sand at the same time. Turning to look, he saw them emerge. They were as white as the sand they dwelled in, and almost as small. He saw them swarm up the dragon's body, easily identifiable against her onyx scales.

Drakthira roared and rose to her feet. Smoke was already pouring out of her nostrils. She began to scorch the sand surrounding them, her dragonfire so hot it melted the sand instantly. Trakon, atop her back, watched the small horde as it traveled up her body. They would be on him soon.

He looked down and saw the melted sand and an idea came to him. Channeling as much of his magic as he could, he reformed the scorched earth, cooling it until it was smooth, smoky glass, then he leapt from Drakthira's back to stand on his newly made platform of glass. As he suspected, the little insects could not climb it, it was too slippery.

The swarm on Drakthira was also not making any progress. Her scales were much too hard for them to break through, and her wounds from the Myste were long since healed. Still, he worried they might make it inside of her mouth or nostrils once she stopped breathing fire.

"Sylas, the pack! Bring it to me!" he said.

Obediently, the dog raced to where he had left their bag of supplies. Remaining *dim*, except for his head, he snatched up the strap in his mouth and hurried back to the old man.

Trakon took the bag and began to sort through it as fast as he could. The first thing he saw was the small vial containing the tear from the Whisperwood, and he hesitated. He had no doubt she could handle this situation, but he didn't want to utilize the tear unless he absolutely had to. Besides, truth be told, he was more afraid of the Whisperwood than he was of the insects.

Finally, after a few minutes of searching, his hand closed on a piece of tree bark. He had picked it up along the way, fascinated at the shape of a spider caught within a small circle of hardened tree sap stuck to its rough surface. He tightened his hand around the piece of wood, letting himself feel the tiny kernel of life nearly extinguished within the wood. He coaxed it out, stretching it to reach the spider trapped inside its amber prison, then threw it, hard, to the ground where it hit the glass and shattered.

The newly freed spider seemed disoriented, but quickly recovered. Trakon could feel its hunger as it seized first one, then another, and another of the little white insects. Knowing the single spider wouldn't be enough, Trakon focused again and used the growing life force within the insect to duplicate the first, until there were two spiders chasing down the horde of miniscule, white bugs. Being so light themselves, they didn't attract the attention of the swarm like Drakthira or himself.

Trakon repeated the process, duplicating the spiders until there were hundreds, then thousands of large, black spiders. Some were incinerated in Drakthira's fire, but most steered clear of the heat and chased down the bothersome white horde that had swarmed the dragon, as well as the ones still emerging from the sand.

Sooner than he expected, the remaining white insects disappeared back in the sand, the spiders dispersing as they chased after them. Trakon knelt and picked up a piece of the shattered tree sap. Holding it within his hands, he magically transformed it back into a more malleable, claylike consistency.

Drakthira had stopped breathing fire and Trakon realized the ground they stood on was now dark, smoky glass for yards around where he stood. 'Thira stepped up onto the glass platform, not wanting to attract another swarm of bugs.

"Here, 'Thira, let me make sure all of the bugs are off of you," Trakon said, showing her the sticky sap in his hand. He could tell she wasn't thrilled with the idea, but caution won out, and she nodded her head once, briefly.

"It won't be too bad. I will stretch this out over your entire body, then harden it so you can simply shake it off. All the remaining bugs should get caught within, like the spider was before. Now, close your eyes."

Drakthira stood still while Trakon worked, her eyes tightly closed. She felt the sap spread over her body, warm and sticky, before suddenly hardening into a thin, hard shell. Once hardened, the sap felt restrictive on her scales and she immediately flexed, shaking as she did so, and felt the sap crack and fall away.

"See, that wasn't too bad," Trakon said soothingly.

'Thira just snorted. He hadn't been covered in sap, after all. *You did well, wizard. Thank you,* she said graciously.

"You are very welcome, of course," the old man said. "I guess now I understand why there are so many bones lying around. I thought the animals must have simply drunk the water, but now I'm not so sure."

Are there more of them? Under the sand?

Trakon felt for the presence of more of the bugs hidden within the sand. He didn't feel any in their immediate vicinity, but as he stretched his senses out further, he could feel them everywhere, *surrounding* them.

"Yes, 'Thira," he said, barely whispering now, as if the sound of his voice would bring them back. "There are many out there, surrounding us. The sand is full of them."

We should be safe here, upon the glass. Until Dax returns, she said, curling up on the glass.

Trakon nodded absently. Now that he was aware of the creatures in the sand, he couldn't be unaware. He settled himself on the glass and stared out over the sand, feeling the tiny lifeforms milling about and knowing it would take only the slightest disturbance to bring them swarming up again. He barely noticed when Sylas lay down beside him, putting his massive head in the old man's lap.

Trakon absently scratched the dog's ears while he stared out into the white nothingness surrounding them, listening to their captors hidden in the sand. He hoped Dax returned soon.

Chapter Eight

Monsters are real, and ghosts are real too. They live inside us, and sometimes, they win.

~ Stephen King

Daxon soared over a sea of white sand. As far as he could see, nothing stirred, and not even a raven's hoarse *caw!* broke the silence. In some ways it reminded him of the Myste with its desolate landscape, deathly silence, and the constant feeling of danger that permeated the air. Many times he had come close to turning back to his friends, but he kept going, knowing the best way to help them would be for him to find the other side of this wasteland and teleport them away from it.

It had been at least five hours since he left. He could no longer see the shore of the lake, just the white, sandy desert that surrounded it. He must be close to the edge of the desert, for it had been at least three hours since he had seen a glimpse of the lake, and according to Trakon, the desert didn't stretch too far from the water's edge. Of course, like everything in Darkenfel, that, too, could have changed.

Dusk was beginning to settle over the land when Dax finally saw the edge of the desert on the horizon. From his vantage point above, Dax could see the land sloped upward around a shallow depression that housed the sand of the desert he had just traversed. A small, fox-like creature was running along the ridge that separated the desert from what looked to be a field of grass and small, scraggly bushes. The reddish creature flushed out some sort of small rodent, although Dax couldn't make out what it was from this distance, and a zig-zag race for survival ensued.

Coming closer, Dax was able to see it was a young prairie dog the fox was after, and just as he reached them, the little rodent lost its footing in the shifting sand along the ridge and tumbled over the edge. Immediately it began to run away from where the fox still stood atop the ridge, its feet kicking up small tufts of grit as it ran.

Dax expected the fox to follow the rodent into the depression. It would have been easy to catch; it wasn't making very fast progress in the unstable sand. Instead, to his surprise, the fox turned away from its prospective meal and trotted away across the field. This odd behavior stirred curiosity in Dax as he continued to soar above, watching the prairie dog silently struggle to regain its footing and return to the ridge.

Suddenly the small beast emitted a high-pitched squeal and seemed to turn a ghastly white. It started at its feet, and moved upward until there was no trace of the brown fur remaining. Surprised, Dax flew closer, careful not to get too close, and with the last of the sun's rays, he saw there were tiny, white insects swarming over the still living rodent. It writhed under the onslaught and opened its mouth once more to let out a shrill squeaking noise, but it was quickly cut off as the insect horde swarmed into its mouth. Horrified, Dax watched as the small creature was devoured within a matter of seconds. It happened so quickly the little animal's skeletal paws continued to thrash a few seconds after the bugs disappeared back into the sand.

Fear for his friends ran down his spine like a cold waterfall. He had left them upon the white sand, which he now realized was full of tiny, carnivorous predators. He quickly reached out through his bond with 'Thira and was reassured when he felt her presence.

'Thira, is everyone ok? he asked her.

Yes, although I wouldn't land on the sand if I were you, she responded. He could feel her disgust through their connection.

I am at the edge of the desert. I will find a place to camp, and then come get you all, he told her. He shared with her the image of the prairie dog's fate. In return, she showed him what had transpired since he had been gone. He was grateful Trakon had identified the danger before the insects had a chance to swarm them. He laughed out loud when 'Thira showed him an image of Trakon covering her with tree sap. He could feel her irritation at being covered with the sticky substance, but he understood the need.

Back soon, he said as he soared over the grassy plain looking for a place that would offer some shelter against the wind and any wild animals in the vicinity. They didn't need any more surprises.

Miles away from Dax and the other members of the party, in the very center of the salt filled lake, was a small island shrouded from view by thick, yellowish-green vapors that arose from the surrounding water. Over the years many flying creatures had attempted to fly over the lake, misjudging the expansive length of it, only to fall from the sky, exhausted. They quickly succumbed to the poison surrounding them, their thirst so intense they drank from the waters and hurried the death already stalking them. Unlike the waters by the shore, these waters were filled with bodies in various states of decay, and most appeared to have been fed upon.

Many, many years ago, the lake had been home to a large colony of water nymphs that lived in harmony with a great population of mer-people. One of the nymphs fell in love with a merman, and even changed her own appearance to that of a mermaid so they could be together. The other nymphs protested at first, not out of spite, but because nymphs were not supposed to experience emotions like mortals, and they feared for her. Over time they forgot their fears as their sister and the merman lived in bliss, deeply in love, and no harm befell their beloved sister.

Centuries passed and the merman began to show signs of aging. Slight at first, it still bothered the nymph-turned-mermaid, and she approached her sisters and asked if they would grant her mate the gift of immortality. This was a serious request, for every year granted to the merman would take a year from some other creature, and the carefree nymphs did not want to take on such a heavy burden. Instead, they tried to reason with their sister, telling her stories about how much fun it would be once she could return to being a nymph and no longer had to pose as a mermaid. She would always have memories of her beloved mate, but she could once more return to her immortal, carefree life.

Unappeased, their sister left them to their twittering laughter. To this point, the only mortal emotion she had felt was love for the merman, but another mortal emotion crept into her heart at her sisters' refusal; resentment. Unable to do anything without her sisters' help, the nymph watched as her beloved mate continued to age, while she stayed young and beautiful, growing more bitter with each passing year. Finally, she sat with her husband on his deathbed, tears streaming down her face as she listened to him take his last breath, his once strong hand falling from her own.

Just as the last breath left his body, her sisters appeared, gently grasping her hand and coaxing her to come back to them. They were distraught over her tears, never having known sadness or heartbreak, they did not know what to do. Unable to mollify their sister's heartbreak, they eventually fled from her to escape the waves of despair emanating from their beloved sister.

The nymph-turned-mermaid was unable to stop her tears, and for many years she lived alone in a small underwater cave, mourning her lost love. After a century had passed, she began to remember the joy she had felt dancing on the water with her sisters, bathing in the waterfall, reveling in the sunlight that warmed her naked body. She yearned to return to that carefree life and tried to return to her nymph form. At first, her body didn't respond, but at last she stirred the magic that had been long-dormant within her body, and tapped into it. She made another attempt to return to the nymph she had once been, and this time she succeeded in changing her appearance, but not as she intended.

Instead of the beautiful, blue-skinned, green-haired young nymph she had been, her magic transformed her body to match the bitterness she had felt all these years. She watched as the shimmering blue scales covering her mermaid tail were replaced with dull, grey skin, until her tail resembled that of a shark. The human part of her torso, once tan and healthy, now appeared pale and sickly. Her once proud, young breasts now began to sag and dry up, and her lustrous, green hair was shriveled and began to fall out until she was completely bald. Seeing her reflection in the water, she gasped to find that her beautiful white teeth had now become sharp as needles, and her eyes were dark and empty as the deepest pools.

The once-beautiful nymph was furious at her sisters, blaming them for what she had become, and furious they had denied her wish to forever live in love with her mate. Screaming in anger and despair, she left her cavern, determined that her sisters would pay, but when she emerged, they were nowhere to be found.

She swam to the mermaid village, but found it deserted. Not a single fish could be found. Distraught, with tears still streaming from her now murky orbs, she went in search of her sisters, eventually finding them lounging quietly at the water's edge.

"What has happened?" she asked. "Where is everyone?"

Her sisters looked at her, but there was no joy in their eyes, only disgust at her ugly appearance. "They have left, dear sister. Nothing lives in this lake anymore," one said, idly making shapes in the water with her finger, refusing to meet her eyes.

"But… why?" she asked.

"It's too salty to support life now," another nymph answered. "Your tears have polluted it over the years, and now only we remain."

"We were just getting ready to leave but wanted to tell you first. We go to find another lake to make beautiful, where we can once again dance and bring happiness. We didn't want to leave you behind, but as you are no longer one of us, we cannot take you with us. Farewell, sister." And with that, the nymphs who remained got to their feet and began walking away, leaving the nymph-turned-monster to herself, alone in the salty lake.

The former nymph watched as her past sisters rose, marching off, not even looking back at her. Her rage bubbled back to the surface and before she realized what she was doing, she lunged and grabbed one of the few remaining nymphs, squeezing her until her eyes bulged from her beautiful face, and her blue tinted skin turned grey, then purple.

"You will not just toss me aside like I don't matter!" she hissed in the nymph's terrified face. "Do you understand? You will stay here with me! You will not leave me alone!"

As she ranted, she drew the nymph closer and closer to her face, shaking the small woman to emphasize her point. Uncontrollable rage shook through her body at the nymph's struggle to be released. She could smell the fear rolling off the little blue frame, and it excited her. The former nymph inhaled her sister's fear deeply, intoxicated by the smell of a mortal emotion emanating from an immortal body. Her mouth began to water, and without thinking, she bit the head off of the struggling nymph, drinking deeply of the dying creature's blood, clear as the water she once danced upon.

When the tiny body was drained of blood and her hunger wore off, realization of what she had done washed through her, and she gagged in disgust at her own actions. She had killed and eaten a living creature! And, not just any creature, but a nymph, her sister! What had she done?! Horror and despair overcame her, and as her eyes spilled tears, the lake became even more polluted.

Alone, and with nowhere to go, the former nymph retreated back to her underwater cavern, hiding from the world. Eventually, however, her hunger came again, and she remembered the way her sister's blood had tasted, the way the fear and terror had smelled. She left her cavern and swam to a nearby bed of algae. This had been her favorite algae to eat when she had been a nymph. They hadn't needed to eat, but the algae had been so good, and you could taste the sunshine caught within. She brought a handful up to her mouth.

She choked down a mouthful, but was unable to stomach any more. It no longer tasted like sunshine; it tasted like cold, dank sludge in her mouth. This would not satisfy her hunger.

The sound of a twig snapping caught her attention, and when she spun around she saw a tree dyad gathering water from the lake for her precious tree. Quickly, she slipped beneath the surface of the water and swam towards the dryad, meaning to talk to the little lady and hopefully make a friend. Now that her sisters were gone and she knew no one else lived in the lake, she felt very alone.

Swimming to within a few feet of the dryad, she waited for it to dip its bucket into the lake again, then she leaped from the water, catching the small, green woman up in her claw-tipped hands. The little lady saw her empty, black eyes and pale skin and began to scream, struggling to get away.

"It's ok, it's me, I'm a nymph," she tried to explain, but the dryad wasn't listening. It screamed in its tiny voice. Fear was emanating off its green body, the smell intoxicating to the former nymph. She found herself poking the little green being with her claws, just enough to puncture the skin, to heighten her fear. Saliva flooded her mouth, and when she could no longer stand it, she bit the head off the dryad and drank her blood, then tore the little corpse into bite-sized pieces and devoured the rest of it.

When her meal was finished, reality set in once more. Although she still cried, it was more from habit than sadness now. The immortals were little more than food now, and she understood they could not be her friends. Her sisters had been right; she was no longer a nymph. She was… something else. Something that fed on nymphs. Something twisted and deformed that should never have been.

As time passed and word spread, fewer and fewer creatures visited the salty shores of the lake whose real name was long forgotten. Now it was known as Salt Crystal Lake, a place to be avoided… a place devoid of life. But unbeknownst to any but the oldest living residents of Darkenfel, there was one that still lived on a small island in the center of the murky waters, though it slept. Over the years it had devoured anything living surrounding the lake until it became a white, sandy wasteland.

Now its sleep had been disturbed. Rising, it sniffed the air, funneling out the putrid smells surrounding it. It peeled its lips back in a smile, revealing sharp, grotesque teeth. Its eyes ran with tears, leaving dark trails down its somewhat humanoid face. Quietly, it slithered into the brittle water and swam swiftly towards the southeastern shore, cutting through the thick water effortlessly. Visitors had come once more to her shores.

And she was hungry.

Chapter Nine

There are very few monsters who warrant the fear we have of them.

~ Andre Gide

Drakthira awoke from a light nap. It had been at least an hour since she had spoken to Dax through their shared bond and her first thought was that something had happened to him, causing her to unexpectedly awaken. She felt for her bond-mate ever so lightly, not enough to even make him aware of her presence, but more like a whispered touch. He was still looking for a suitable place to camp and seemed untroubled. He was not the reason she had awakened.

A slight turn of her head revealed Trakon slouched over Sylas' prone body, both of them snoring loudly. Smirking, she concluded their snoring must have been what had disturbed her sleep, and was preparing to go back to sleep when she felt it again.

Rising, she walked to the edge of the glass, careful not to allow even a single claw to disturb the salty sand, and stared off towards the west. Something was out there. Something powerful. It called to her in a distant voice, as if it were only now awakening fully, only now aware of her existence. She felt its presence focus on her, heavy and lingering, for just a few moments. And then it was gone.

Growling low in her throat, Drakthira searched for the presence again but was unable to find it. She couldn't sense whether it was friend or foe, but she was reasonably sure that each of them was equally aware of the other's presence. More than that, she was sure it had come from the west, the direction Dax had gone.

Her scales clattered in agitation as she paced back and forth along the edge of the glass, trying to determine what to do. Daxon didn't seem to be in danger, and she didn't want to leave Sylas and Trakon alone. She could wake them and allow Trakon to ride upon her back, but she didn't know how much farther it was across the desert and she feared having to land in the bug infested sand if she grew too tired.

111

A small skittering noise caught her attention and she looked down at the glass under her feet. The little white bugs were following her movement from underneath the glass, their bodies sliding along it as their legs searched for purchase. She could see where her heavy footsteps had squished some of them against the glass, but their companions were quick to devour all trace of their deaths. Fascinated by their mindless persistence, 'Thira walked slowly across the glass, watching as the swarm of hungry insects felt her movements and followed her step by step. After a few moments, she became bored by this distraction and once more her gaze turned west.

The presence was gone and if she had been human, she would have questioned if it had simply been her imagination, but, being a dragon, she had no such doubts. It troubled her to think it may still be out there, shielding its presence from her, for how else could it have disappeared so quickly? It hadn't felt like it was particularly close, but that did little to quell her worry. A being able to make its presence known across a vast distance must truly be powerful indeed.

'Thira found herself pacing once more. She was so focused on her thoughts she didn't notice Sylas until she almost walked right into him. He was standing at the edge of the glass, as she had been just moments before, gazing westward out into the night. He turned his head to look at her, his small, stubby tail wagging slowly for just a moment before he turned away again, his ears alert for any sound.

The young dragon turned her head to stare in the same direction as the dog, also listening. Now that she was no longer pacing, she could hear a slight *swishing* sound coming from the darkness. She hadn't been able to hear it before over the sound of her claws clicking on the glass. Now that she did hear it, she realized it didn't sound like something walking on the sand, but more like something moving through it or over it in a swimming or slithering motion.

She looked down through the glass beneath her feet. The small, white insects were gone. She expected at any moment to hear the sounds of a struggle as they attacked this new intruder, but as the moments passed the only sound she heard was the *swishing* getting closer.

The creature circled the group which lay upon what looked like a flat pane of glass. Although she was no longer a nymph, she still retained some of their powers, including the ability to glide through water faster than thought, and with a slight adaptation, through sand just as quickly. It had not taken her long to arrive at the eastern edge of the lake, her keen sense of smell leading her straight to the human, dragon, and dog she now regarded. Her shriveled, grey tongue peeked out from her lips and ran over her lips in anticipation of the taste of blood. It had been so long since she had tasted fresh meat.

Circling cautiously, she remained hidden in the darkness. The air surrounding the party smelled of fire and magic. The fire she easily chalked up to the dragon and it explained why the insects which lived in the surrounding sands had not devoured the intruders. The dragon must have created the glass by melting the sand, a clever trick.

She knew the insects would not bother her, would have, in fact, fled from her presence. As the lake had dried up and the salt from her tears had created the vast desert, the bugs had just appeared. At first, they had attacked her, and more than a few times she had fled from them, back into the salty, brittle waters of the lake. But, over time, she had learned they could not tolerate water and remained a healthy distance from the shore. The last time they had attacked her she had nearly killed the entire swarm simply by calling forth water and allowing it to run down her body and into the sand, an easy enough task for a water nymph, even a former one. After that, they had fled from her.

Focusing her attention back on the group, she saw the dragon and dog looking in her direction, following the sounds of her movement. She didn't know if they could actually see her, but it was obvious they were aware something was out in the darkness. She had never fought a dragon, had not even seen a dragon in many, many years. Nor had she ever seen a dog like the one she now watched. Whereas the dragon smelled of brimstone and death, the dog simply smelled like clouds laden with rainwater, but she was sure there was more to him than that. The former nymph had never been away from the lake and the smell of the Myste's magic coursing through Sylas was foreign to her, but she knew instinctively he was more dangerous than he appeared.

The human would be the easiest target. He was still asleep, close to the edge of the pane of glass, although far enough back so he wouldn't accidentally touch the sand in his sleep. She was sure if she could just distract the dragon and the dog long enough, she could drag the man away and once in the water, they would have no chance of catching her.

Just as a plan began to form in her mind, the night sky seemed to catch on fire, and a tremendous roar shook the ground underneath her.

'Thira and Sylas traced the progress of the thing out in the sand by the slithering sounds it made. After realizing the meat-eating bugs in the sand were not going to attack it, they waited to see when it would show itself. That it was dangerous was not in question. And although neither knew exactly what it was, they could smell its foul stench of decaying meat and brine.

Briefly, Drakthira wondered if this was the presence she had felt earlier, but she pushed the thought aside. Even if it was, she would not back down from the threat, would not allow it to harm Trakon or Sylas if she could stop it. She drew in deep breaths, allowing her fire to burn up through her belly, feeling it gather in the back of her throat. Her spine spikes stood at full attention along her back, and the trident-like set of blades on her tail also made themselves known. She was ready.

By her estimation, the creature had already circled the glass one full turn and was currently on its second. The waiting was infuriating, especially when waiting on something unseen and unknown. The fire within her was seeking release, it felt like a hot, tight knot in the back of her mouth, but still she breathed deeply, feeding it and allowing it to grow larger, burn hotter. When it felt like she could no longer contain it, she took a last deep breath and with a roar like rolling thunder, she spewed the white-hot fire in an arc in front of her, in the direction she knew the creature to be.

The sound woke Trakon and he sprang to his feet. The fire's glow allowed each of them to see for the first time the grotesque beast stalking them. And *grotesque* was a kind word indeed, for the creature's body was covered with dull, gray skin which culminated in a distorted, shark-like tail. The mysterious *swishing* sound 'Thira had heard earlier was the creature's tail moving back and forth like a snake, propelling it forward. Now it stood, frozen, with lifeless black eyes that contained no light to reflect back to the fire. Thick, watery tears rolled from the black pools, down its cheeks until they fell, heavily, to the sand below. Its lips were peeled back to reveal razor sharp, triangular teeth, stained from years of subsisting on decayed matter.

Trakon felt like he was back in the Myste once more, his still sleepy mind trying to comprehend how this monstrosity had managed to escape and follow them here. Trying to grasp some sense of reality, his eyes kept going back to the creature's nose, which was pert and very human-like and seemed completely out of place on such an ugly visage.

Drakthira launched herself at their stalker, but was quickly taken aback when the thing burrowed under the sand as if it were water. For a moment, she could see a triangular fin cutting through the sand like a finely-honed cleaver before it, too, disappeared. She searched for some sign of the creature in the sand around her, but all seemed quiet. She kept her back to the pane of glass Trakon and Sylas were still standing upon, confident they would shout out a warning if the creature reappeared, while she searched the sand in front of her.

Minutes ticked by and still the slithering creature did not show itself. Drakthira was reluctant to lower her guard, knowing the beast was still out there somewhere. She started to walk back to the safety of the glass in case the carnivorous insects decided to come back. She had only taken a few steps when the sand suddenly shifted beneath her front foot and, looking down, she saw the thing's eyes looking up at her, its lips peeled back in a snarl. Before she could take a breath, its arm appeared out of the sand and a hand clasped over the front of her muzzle.

A bubble of water instantly formed over her mouth and nostrils, immediately cutting off her ability to breathe. 'Thira tried to pierce it with her claws, but the mucous-covered bubble was very strong, and her feet only managed to slide down the surface.

Desperately, she tried opening her maw, but the bubble stretched with the movement and water began to flow down her throat. She quickly snapped her mouth shut and shook her head viciously from side to side in an attempt to dislodge the bubble from her snout. Nothing worked.

Trakon, seeing Thira's distress, ran out onto the sand to help her, all thoughts of the white sand bugs forgotten. He tried to grasp the bubble and pull it off her face, but like her claws, his hands simply slid away. Deciding to try a different tactic, he reached out with his magic and tried to pierce the bubble or at the very least, dislodge it, but his magic seemed to simply fizzle whenever it came close to the watery orb. It was apparent to him the creature's magic was quite powerful, and there simply wasn't enough life energy in this barren place for him to gather force sufficient to combat it.

In a desperate attempt to help his dragon friend, Trakon searched for a sharp stick or a shard of glass to try and puncture the bubble, knowing in his heart it wouldn't work, but unwilling to give up. He saw Sylas out of the corner of his eye standing between the now fully revealed creature and Drakthira, growling and snapping ferociously. The beast didn't seem to know how to get past the huge dog. Trakon watched as the beast lunged at Sylas, who instantly dissolved into his mist form. The dog's form held a greenish tint to it, and when the creature's clawed hand came in contact, it instantly snatched it away, but not before Trakon saw the flesh being stripped away. It reminded him of when Dax had first met Sylas and the dog had tried to play with him, but had inadvertently stripped his arm of flesh within seconds. The creature's flesh was not as easily devoured as Daxon's had been then, but it was obviously vulnerable to Sylas' Myste magic.

Seeing the reaction the creature was having to Sylas, Trakon wondered if the large dog's magic could destroy the watery bubble. He opened his mouth to shout out to his companion, but before he could speak, chaos broke free.

Drakthira collapsed, unmoving, the bubble still stuck tightly over her mouth and nose. At the same moment she fell, the remaining three were distracted by a loud *crack* that seemed to come from the west. The sound seemed to hang in the air, almost tangible, before being followed moments later by a dense wind full of dust and bits of flying rock.

Trakon was sure that the roar that followed shook all of Darkenfel. Sylas dissipated, but Trakon and the creature were both thrown to the ground, their hands clasped to their ears. The old wizard could feel the anger and ferocity released in the sound, and the fear he felt reminded him of when he stood in the Whisperwood's presence, only perhaps even more terrible.

Finally, the sound ceased, and Trakon realized he could barely see. His eyesight was red and hazy, and when he looked at the creature that was also picking itself up off the ground, he saw its eyes were now ruby colored and filled with blood from burst blood vessels, and quickly understood. He blinked several times to try and clear his vision, but soon forgot about it as a monstrous shape blocked out all light, and darkness fell.

Chapter Ten

The death of a beloved is an amputation.

~ C.S. Lewis

Daxon had been flying over the grassy plains searching for a safe place to set up camp for the night, but the plains were wide open and offered little in the way of shelter or concealment. Although the grasses were waist high to him, they would do little to conceal Drakthira's towering height, so on he flew, ever westward.

After an hour or more he realized he was coming to the foothills of the Crimson Peak Mountains. He hadn't realized how close they were once he crossed the white sands. Shrouded in fog, they were hard to see until you were almost upon them. From a distance they merely looked like clouds hanging low in the sky. He picked up his pace as renewed energy surged through him. He would be able to teleport his friends close to their destination and he could finally get some sleep.

Although the night was cloudy, three of Darkenfel's six moons were visible in the sky. Two glowed dimly, one a dark red color and one the color of glowing twilight, but the third was large and bright, emitting a silvery light that gently illuminated Dax's surroundings. He was glad for the light as he searched for a shallow cave or small copse of trees to shelter in for the night. The closer he came to the mountains the more likely it seemed he would be able to find an overhanging rock at least, but the indomitable mountains seemed to hide their secret entrances well.

Dax picked up on a distant rumbling sound and he worried there might be a storm coming, but this storm didn't sound like any other he had ever witnessed. There were no sudden claps of thunder or sharp, jagged lights splitting the sky, but more of a deep rumbling that he could feel in his bones, even in his *dim* form. He slowed to a stop and hovered, cautiously looking around to see if he could pinpoint the source of these odd sounds. Movement off to his left revealed a herd of goat-like creatures charging recklessly down the mountainside, their cloven hooves dislodging loose rocks in their haste to get away.

Although Dax by no means considered himself a wildlife expert, he knew there were mountain goats on Daegonlot as well, and they never came down from their mountainous home. They were, in fact, one of the hardest creatures to hunt due to their nimble and fearless leaps and bounds at staggering heights. He peered up the mountain to see what had caused these goats to abandon their home, but he could see nothing chasing them.

A sense of dread ran down Daxon's spine. The rumbling was becoming louder and it seemed like the very mountain itself was trembling in fear of the unseen entity. *What does a mountain fear?* Dax thought, his mind racing wildly. Any other time he would consider the thought ridiculous, but at this moment it seemed very reasonable, indeed. The very air he hovered felt like it was waiting for a momentous occurrence to take place, as if the world of Darkenfel were holding its breath in anticipation.

As abruptly as it had begun, all sound ceased. The seconds drew themselves out, hanging heavy in time, and every detail felt burned into Daxon's mind. The light from the moons above shimmered over the plains, turning the rich, green grass into a field of silvery, dancing lights as it swayed gently. He blinked, the movement seeming to take three times as long as normal, as if he, too, were caught in some sort of slow motion, trapped in a place where time seemed reluctant to pass.

Caught in this surreal moment, he looked skyward and watched as newly fallen raindrops slowly fell towards his upturned face. The perfectly formed droplets looked to have captured bits of the moon's brilliance and were struggling to bring it to the ground below. Distantly, Dax realized he had never fully appreciated the beauty of rain, and he reached out to touch one of the drops now slowly falling directly in front of him. The tip of his finger made contact with it. The small drop broke and spilled forth its minuscule bounty of water and moonlight.

The tiny catastrophe broke whatever spell had come over Dax, whether real or imagined, and sound came rushing back in. A sharp clap of thunder assaulted his ears, followed by a horrendously loud groaning that came from the mountain itself. He heard the rumbling again, but it no longer sounded distant. Seemed, in fact, to be gaining volume and momentum. For a brief second, the rumbling suddenly stopped, and shortly thereafter a terrifying roar took its place.

Dax watched in horrified fascination as the mountain began to sway. In the dim light of the moons he could barely make out the crimson peaks for which the mountains were named, and they seemed to be moving, somehow becoming longer and undulating all along the mountain peaks as far as he could see. The mountain itself shuddered, as if it were struggling to contain whatever was trapped within it.

Without warning, the mountain exploded out in a rush of wind, rocks, and dust. The force of the blast knocked Dax backwards through the air, but over the roar of the wind he heard a last, triumphant shriek before a dark, inky form blotted out all light from the sky. Keeping his arm up to shield his eyes, Dax just barely made out glowing red eyes before the beast was gone, moving at tremendous speed.

Unsure of what he had just witnessed, Dax reached out to Drakthira through their bond to warn her of the possible threat coming their way. He could feel her presence on the other end, but it was weak, and quickly fading away. Fear greater than anything he had ever felt clutched his heart as reality sank in.

Drakthira was dying.

Rapidly blinking his eyes, Trakon managed to clear them enough to see clearly, albeit with a pinkish tint. In the muted silvery light of the moons above he was able to see the monstrous form before him, but it wasn't until the great beast lowered its head to the shark-tailed creature from the sands did he truly understand what he was seeing. With a gasp he realized it was a dragon, a true giant of its kind, with flaming ruby eyes and teeth longer than his entire body.

The great dragon seized the now terrified creature in its maw, crunching down and cutting off its last attempts at escaping under the sand. With a toss of its massive head, the dragon threw the lifeless body into the air, catching it and swallowing it whole, and putting an end to its pitiful existence.

Unsure if this new dragon was a friend or foe, Trakon moved with slow, cautious steps towards Drakthira. The bubble covering her snout had disappeared with the death of the former nymph, but her ability to breathe had not been restored. He had gone but a few steps when the massive head swung towards him, and the ruby eyes bore into his own. He froze in terror, his mind at war with itself. He wanted to turn and check on his fallen friend, but he was terrified to turn his back to the newcomer.

Sylas appeared directly in front of him, a low growl deep in his chest issuing forth from his snarling muzzle. A second later Trakon heard an anguished cry; "Drakthira!" He turned to see Dax kneeling over 'Thira's prone body, her head cradled gently in his lap. "No, 'Thira, please, come back! Wake up!"

Move aside, thundered through Dax and Trakon's mind as the huge dragon stretched out his (from the voice, there was no doubt left in their minds it was a male dragon) neck until his mouth hovered right above Drakthira's still form. After a few long seconds had passed, a small, yellow-orange filament of light issued forth from the beast's giant jaws and entered 'Thira's mouth and nostrils. Time stood still for Dax, yet as the seconds passed her entire body seemed to be bathed in the muted glow, then it disappeared and she took her first, gasping breath.

"Thank you," Dax said. He rubbed 'Thira's eye ridges, then threw his arms around her neck and hugged her tightly. The young dragon accepted the hug, even nuzzling the top of his head and purring contentedly. *It is good to see you again, too,* she said so only he could hear.

"I hate to break this up," Trakon began, "but we should probably get off of this sand before those bugs decide to come back."

The human is right, but we have much to discuss. The young dragon needs to rest. Climb upon my back. We will be safe in my lair.

"Who are you?" Dax asked, uncertainty clear in his voice. This behemoth may have saved his bond-mate, and for that he was eternally grateful, but he still didn't know if they should trust the newcomer.

It's alright, Dax. Let's go with him. He means us no harm.

The elf looked into his bond-mate's eyes and, after a moment, nodded his agreement. He trusted her and knew she would never lead him into danger. He motioned for Trakon to mount, then Drakthira, and he brought up the rear. Sylas, too, appeared on the broad back and took a position near Trakon.

As soon as they were all situated between the blood red spines along his back, the giant black dragon leapt into the air, snapping his wings open at the last moment. With powerful thrusts he sped through the air back towards the mountains. Watching the ground pass by in a blur, Dax was amazed at how quickly they arrived at their destination. It had taken him most of a day to get to where they were now in just over half an hour.

The mountain's destruction was clearly visible as they approached. It was now evident to Daxon that the peaks for which the mountains were named had actually been the spine spikes of the dragon upon which they were now riding. When he had burst from his stony tomb, the entire top half of the mountains had been destroyed. Looking down, the party could see the mountains were mostly hollow, almost as if they had formed around the great beast they had once contained.

The great, black dragon landed within the hollow opening and the party quickly dismounted. As soon as they were off his back, the dragon yawned hugely and stretched, his scales clattering loudly as they settled into place.

Forgive me, he said, *it has been many centuries since I was last awake.* He squinted a large, ruby eye at the party. *Do you know who I am, young one?* he finally asked.

Drakthira hesitated, then said, *I do not know who you are, but I feel like I should. I can feel your presence within my very blood, as if it's singing to me.*

The dragon lowered his great head in acknowledgement. *That's because you are my granddaughter, little one.*

"Your granddaughter?!," Dax asked, incredulous. "How can that be possible? You are by far the largest dragon I've ever seen, even larger than 'Thira's mother, and up to now *she* was the largest dragon I'd ever seen! You have got to be... ancient! You... you were a mountain. Like... an actual *mountain!*"

The dragon cocked his head to the side and asked, *A mountain? What do you mean? I have always been a dragon...*

"I don't mean you turned into a mountain," Dax explained. "I mean these mountains," he began, gesturing with his hands to encompass their surroundings, "were named after you. The Crimson Peaks. They weren't peaks at all, they were your spine spikes! If I had to hazard a guess, I would bet you were asleep so long the earth actually grew *around* you, forming these mountains. It's incredible!" he finished, his face clearly showing his awe.

It's hard to believe I slept that long… the dragon said, his eyes showing a profound sadness.

"Why did you sleep that long?" Trakon asked.

The dragon lowered his head until he was as close to eye level with the old man as possible. *Because of* your *kind, human.* He growled menacingly, the sound vibrating through the very ground. Immediately Sylas appeared between the old man and the dragon, his lips pulled back in a snarl as he, too, emitted a somewhat less impressive growl.

Trakon is a good man, and a true friend to dragons, Drakthira said. *As is Sylas.*

"Let's all calm down and take a step back," Dax said. He gestured at the black dragon. "Please, tell us your story from the beginning, starting with your name."

Chapter Eleven

Come back. Even as a shadow, even as a dream.

~ Euripides

My name, the black dragon murmured, looking off to a distant point above their heads. *In my time dragons did not have names.*

"What do you mean you don't have a name? Even the wild dragons have names or else 'Thira's mother would not have told me what to call her," Dax interjected.

Our master did not bestow upon us names, young hybrid. A purpose, yes, but not a name. We were created to be the protectors of Darkenfel, and we did not need names to fulfill that purpose.

"Your master? You are a tame dragon?" Trakon asked, confused.

A terrifying roar shrieked from the beast's great mouth as he thrashed his head angrily from side to side.

Tame dragon? There is no such thing as a 'tame' dragon, human! Only dragons who have been somehow brainwashed into believing they need masters, and no, I was never that, nor will I ever be!

Dax put up his hands in an attempt to placate the angered dragon. "I think what Trakon meant to ask is who your master is."

Franklin is my master, my creator, and the one who tasked me with keeping Darkenfel safe. Myself and the others. But in the end, we all failed. The dragon slumped forward, hanging his head in sorrow and shame.

Darkenfel is still here, ancient one, so you have not failed yet. Please, tell us your story. Maybe we were brought together so we could help. It is our quest to rejoin Daegonlot with Darkenfel, and in so doing save us all, Drakthira gently prodded.

"Did you say Franklin?" Dax asked, incredulous. "As in Franklin and Alexius, the original creators of all life on Darkenfel? You are one of the original dragons?"

Yes, I was one of the first four dragons. Franklin created us to protect Alexius's creations, and Darkenfel itself. For many years it was very easy to do so. So easy, in fact, we all became bored and stopped patrolling the borders, preferring to frolic and play with each other instead. Draogothra, Drakthira's mother, was one of the first generation of dragons native to Darkenfel. She was the daughter of myself and the amethyst dragon, hatched from the very first clutch of dragon eggs to ever touch Darkenfel's soil.

"How are you even still alive?" Dax asked. Then, realizing what he had said, he stammered, "I mean, no disrespect, but I've never known a dragon to live so long. Drakthira's mother had to be the oldest dragon I've ever known of, but even she was nowhere near as large as you."

Draogothra's clutch was hatched many, many years after our creation. To my knowledge, she was the last of her nest-mates still surviving. Time in Darkenfel is quite fluid, so it is hard to pinpoint exactly how old she was. As for how I'm still alive, to understand that you would have to understand dragons. We were created to be protectors. Our reproduction is quite slow compared to other creatures that inhabit this world. As it should be. If we were to overrun Darkenfel, there would not be enough food to sustain a large population. While we are serving our purpose we have a fierce desire to live and can live for as long as we want. But, once we feel we have fulfilled our purpose or no longer have one, we will waste away and die.

"So you don't actually have a set number of years to live. How interesting," Trakon said, mumbling to himself over this new piece of information.

What has been your purpose for all these years, Old One?

The giant black dragon lowered his muzzle and gently brushed it against Drakthira's side, a steady rumbling coming from deep within his belly.

Part of my purpose has been to watch over my progeny. But, that alone would not have sustained me. However, many years ago, so many I do

129

not remember, a young human woman entered my lair. With her, she had a red, glowing orb. I could tell immediately there was very powerful magic within the orb, but imagine my surprise when, upon closer inspection, I found there were dragons captured within that foul ball of light.

"Jessa!" Trakon exclaimed. "You saw her? Do you know if she still lives?"

The ancient dragon regarded Trakon coldly. The old man stumbled back a step under the weight of the black dragon's regard.

Please, Grandfather. Trakon is not our enemy. If you don't trust him, then please, trust me when I tell you this. He has been through many perils with us and has proven himself a trustworthy ally.

The old dragon's gaze lingered a moment longer on Trakon before switching to Drakthira.

As you say, young one. Yes, I have seen the woman you call Jessa, and yes, she is still alive.

When she came into my lair with her ball of light, I saw her well before she ever found me. I saw what she had done, although I did not know the purpose for trapping the dragons within the orb. Not then, anyway.

I watched her as she stumbled around in the dark looking for me. The orb she had concerned me, not only because of the trapped dragons within, but because I could see the power emanating from it, a mixture of dragon magic and something more, something even more powerful. I have since discovered this to be the Blood of the Mountain.

"What is that? This Blood of the Mountain?" Dax asked.

I had the same question, young-Dax. Little did the creators know when they introduced life to Darkenfel. This world itself is alive, and not in the way others are. It's alive… and… aware for lack of a better term. Not aware as you and I, but aware in a much slower, heavier way I guess. When the creators made the Fae, this world became even more aware, as if the existence of other beings awakened it. As the centuries passed, Darkenfel begun collecting small portions of its dying inhabitants. A drop of blood here. A scrap of magic there. Perhaps a bit of bone. I don't know the details, but I do know it compiled these small, stolen pieces and over time, it formed into a pool of ruby red liquid hidden within a mountain.

It was in this pool the woman you speak of emerged into Darkenfel. During her stay underground, before she was allowed free roam of the surface, she drank from this pool many times a day, swam in it, bathed in it, and lived beside it. It somehow changed her, became a part of her, and she now has the power of Darkenfel coursing through her. It was the main source of her power in trapping the dragons within the orb. I believe the orb itself is formed of this power, which is why the dragons cannot break free from it…

"How did you learn all of this?" Dax questioned.

From the woman herself, the dragon said. He rose up slightly on his hind legs and, using one massive claw, removed something from under one of the scales on his belly. Ever so gently, he set it before the small party and stepped back to allow the light to shine upon it.

Trakon gasped as he realized what he was looking at.

Before them was an oval of what looked to be frozen fire. Not entirely translucent, it was still clear enough they could see the form of the woman inside, curled up in a fetal position, her eyes open and staring and her mouth frozen in a terrified scream. In her hand she held a staff they all recognized, but the Dragon Orb was missing from its tip.

"What happened to the Orb?" Dax asked, turning back to the ancient black dragon.

During our fight, when it became apparent to her she may not escape, she sent it away. It now rests under Daegonlot, but it is much too powerful for me to destroy alone.

"What about her?" Trakon asked. "What is wrong with her? And what is this substance she is trapped within?"

It's dragon fire, Drakthira put in. *Crystallized dragon fire.*

The great black dragon nodded his head in approval and confirmation.

You are correct, Granddaughter. As you know, dragon fire can destroy nearly any magic. But, not the Blood. Even my dragon fire, the oldest in this land, could not destroy it. But, it could contain it. During our battle, when this foul woman tried to trap me within her ball of light, in my desperation to escape I bathed her and the orb within my fire. The orb protected her, not a single flame got through to singe her skin. When I realized this, I called forth the hottest fire I could produce and crystallized it around her, but just before it was complete, she released the orb, which disappeared. Once it was gone, the fire licked upon her skin and she shrieked in pain before the crystallization was complete, trapping her like this for all these years.

"Is she aware in there?" Trakon asked, tears in his eyes.

Yes, she is aware, human. The Blood within her sustains her, but it cannot free her. She didn't speak for many moons, but eventually loneliness overcame her and she told me much of what I have told you. Our last conversation was many years ago, however, for I have been asleep, ensuring she does not escape and complete her vile mission against the dragons. Her mind broke long ago from the darkness and loneliness. There is little left of the woman she was.

He looked Drakthira in the eyes and finished, *And that is what has sustained me all these years. My purpose. To ensure the dragons of Daegonlot are not completely enslaved by this woman's evil.*

Trakon ran his hand across the surface of the smooth, crystallized flame coffin that held Jessa. He could see her eyes move to follow the path of his hand and a tear escaped his eye and ran down his cheek. To see the woman he had loved all those years ago in such a predicament and knowing the torment she had been through broke his heart. He held no animosity towards the black dragon; he understood why such a creature, created to protect the world of Darkenfel, would have no compassion for a person such as Jessa. But he had known her before she became the deranged woman hell bent on enslaving dragons and bending them to her will. He had known the kind, loving, scared, naïve woman who had first entered the world.

"Can you release her from the fire?" Daxon asked.

Why would I ever release her? the giant dragon asked, his head cocked to the side like a curious puppy.

"We believe she may be the key to saving Darkenfel," Dax said. "We will need her to undo what she has done. She is the only one we know for sure who can. If we have to try and undo what she has done we will be taking a huge risk. Only she knows exactly how the Orb was created. Only she knows the magic involved, as well as the intent. We stand a much better chance of succeeding if we have her help."

What makes you think she will help you? She has never shown any remorse for what she has done. Not in the many years she has been trapped here. Even asleep I maintained a link with her to make sure she didn't escape, and never have I felt any remorse for her actions.

"She is still our only real hope," Dax began. "Look, you said she was broken. Maybe we can get her fixed. Not just what broke here, but what broke originally to make her want to do what she has done. I know it's a long shot, but it's the best shot we have," he finished.

After a lengthy discussion, Drakthira was finally the one who convinced the ancient dragon to release Jessa. Although he still didn't think she would help undo the damage she had done, he understood the magic of Darkenfel enough to know she truly was their best chance at succeeding. The only condition he had was that he accompany them on their quest so he could keep an eye on the woman and prevent her from doing any more harm. The party readily agreed. Having such a powerful ally could come in handy for more than just trouble with Jessa.

Gathering around the woman trapped within the frozen fire, they all watched as the great black dragon took several deep breaths, the fire within his belly burning so hot they could see its light shining through his scales. After just a few seconds, he bathed the crystal coffin with his intense heat, and shortly after the crystal began to crack, and small fractures marred its smooth surface. After a few short minutes the fractures had created a spider web pattern across the entire surface, and the coffin abruptly disintegrated into dust.

For a moment nobody moved or said anything. They simply stood and stared at the broken, wild-eyed woman lying before them. Her mouth worked, yet no sound escaped, and her eyes darted quickly from one face to the next. When her eyes landed on Trakon he thought he saw a glimmer of recognition, but it was soon gone, replaced by fear when her eyes landed on Drakthira's draconian face.

She tried to scramble away from the young dragon, but in her haste she ran squarely into the ancient black dragon. Looking up at her captor, fear turned to terror, and she finally found her voice long enough to release a blood chilling scream before fainting.

"Looks like we have our work cut out for us," Dax said finally. The party looked around at each other, exchanging uneasy glances at the unconscious woman lying on the floor. Finally, Trakon bent to pick up the prone woman, gently laying her across Drakthira's back.

"Then let's get started," he said quietly.

Epilogue

Trakon stood at the top of one of the remaining peaks of what used to be the Crimson Peak Mountains. Vaguely he wondered what they would be called now when word spread the peaks were gone and a good portion of the mountain range decimated.

He pushed those thoughts from his mind. That's not what he was here for.

Gently he fingered the crystallized tear within his pocket. It had been almost two weeks since they had freed Jessa from her prison. True, she was awake and no longer screamed in terror when she saw a dragon, but aside from this, little progress had been made. Most of her time was spent staring off into the distance for hours at a time, looking at something only she could see. Her eyes were no longer bright and lively as they had been in her past life, years ago when he had known her. Instead, her entire being seemed dim and lost, not even responding when her name was called out loud. She consumed whatever food and drink they gave to her, but not once did she speak, and never showed even the slightest recognition of anyone or anything around her.

Although nobody actually said it, Trakon knew they had all but given up hope on helping the woman. Helping her would be impossible if they couldn't even get through to her. The only progress that had been made was that she no longer screamed and fainted at the sight of a dragon. But in all reality, they were no closer to determining what was wrong with this shell of a woman, or how to go about fixing her.

Once more Trakon ran his finger over the smooth surface of the crystallized tear and thought back to the words the Whisperwood woman had said to him, *"Keep this safe. When the odds seem insurmountable and you see no other way out, throw the tear to the ground. It will summon me, no matter where I am."*

The last thing he wanted to do was summon the Tree whose very presence struck fear within his heart, a fear so overwhelming nothing else could compare. But he couldn't help thinking the Tree was Jessa's only hope. Although he didn't, nay, couldn't, understand the true meaning of the Tree's existence, he knew it (she?) traveled freely along what she had called the 'currents of time.' Maybe she could take them back to the time before Jessa became so… broken.

Trakon suppressed his fear and doubts. He could see no other way to help Jessa. He knew his biggest concern should be the quest to free the dragons of Daegonlot from the Orb, and it still was, but he had no intentions of leaving the woman he used to love a broken shell of herself if he didn't have to. Before he could change his mind, he threw the tear to the ground and took a quick, involuntary step backward.

For a long moment nothing happened. Trakon, thinking the tear must not have worked, took a step forward to pick it up from the ground where he could see it glittering in the early morning sunlight. Before he could pick it up, however, he felt a faint rumbling beneath his feet and had just enough time to leap backwards before the ground ripped open and the Whisperwood Tree surged from the destroyed earth.

The Tree's form was one he had never seen before, and its beauty took his breath away. Clear crystal leaves clung to branches of gold, silver, and bronze, each metallic limb looking as if it had been crafted by a skilled metal-worker and braided together. The Whisperwood woman, this time covered in a garment of light gold, once more sat in the forked branches. Once the Tree had fully emerged, she leapt lightly to the ground and stood before Trakon.

Without preamble, she asked, "Of all the infinite possibilities you could have used my tear for, why this one?"

"Because I love her," Trakon said simply, unapologetically.

The Whisperwood woman's eyes grew distant, and Trakon was sure she must be looking into the future, at least as far as she was able.

Finally, her eyes came back into focus and she asked, "And what would you ask of me?"

"We can't get Jessa to respond to anything. She is still our best hope of saving Darkenfel. Allow us to travel back to the time and place where it all went wrong for her and she became bitter and angry. Give me the chance to fix it," he pleaded.

Once more the Whisperwood woman's eyes lost focus, but this time, as Trakon watched, the color in her eyes seemed to expand, until both of her eyes were inky black. Images began to flicker across her dark orbs, so quickly Trakon was unable to make out much of what he was seeing, until he finally turned his eyes away to avoid the confusing sight.

Finally, the Whisperwood woman said, "I will grant your wish."

"Thank y…" Trakon began, but he was quickly cut off.

"Don't thank me just yet. Be warned, Earth wizard, the path you have chosen stands little chance for success. All of you must go: Drakthira, Daxon, Sylas, and the original Black dragon, as well as yourself. A black dragon will be the reason this endeavor fails or succeeds. Bonds will be tested and one of your friends will not make it back to this time again. That is all I can tell you on that," she finished.

Trakon nodded his understanding, his mind racing.

"I didn't think your magic affected the dragons," he said, remembering the Whisperwood's words to him in the Myste.

"It doesn't. The dragons can travel the currents of time themselves. But they must be willing to do so, for I cannot make them," she said.

Once more, Trakon nodded his understanding.

"I will meet you here in three days' time," the Whisperwood woman said. Then she was gone. Trakon blinked, looking around, but even the Tree had disappeared without its usual fanfare, leaving him alone once more.

He looked back towards the ruined Crimson Peak Mountains, back towards his friends. The Whisperwood woman's words rang once more in his head; *"one of your friends will not make it back to this time again…"*

Sadness welled up in him, and tears stung his eyes. It seemed no matter which direction he tried to go he would end up losing someone. On the one hand, if he did nothing, Jessa was lost, and possibly Darkenfel as well. But on the other hand, if the others could be convinced to go back with the Whisperwood in time, he would lose one of his friends, but Darkenfel might be saved.

Keeping that thought in his mind, Trakon decided then and there he would keep what the Whisperwood woman said to himself. He didn't know which of their party would not be returning, so he saw no reason to alarm everyone. At least, that's what he told himself.

Reluctantly, he started the long walk back to the Black dragon's lair. He would explain his idea to the others and convince them it was the only way. He had to.

For Jessa. And for Darkenfel.

Acknowledgements

Thank you for journeying with me through Darkenfel once more, and thank you for reading! I can't express my gratitude enough for all the fans that have emailed me, messaged me on Facebook or tweeted me to tell me how much they like my books. It means the world to me.

I'd also like to apologize for the amount of time it took to get this book completed. I had a lot of emails and messages asking when it would be available, and I missed the date I wanted to publish completely. I have moved to a new state and started a new life. It's a journey, and not one we always have a good road map for, but wish me luck!

If you would like to keep up with the Dragons of Daegonlot series, or provide feedback, a review on Amazon is always appreciated.

You can also follow me on Twitter: @shanlynnwalker

Or send me an email: shanlynnwalker@gmail.com.

Or follow me on Facebook:
www.facebook.com/shanlynnwalker

Special thanks to:

My children. They have been an inspiration for these stories, as well as for me as a person. Love you guys!

My boyfriend and his daughter, for helping me out with some names and ideas.

My fur-baby, Sylas, for being awesome enough to inspire one of my main characters. You are such a good boy!!

And, to you, the reader, for reading my books! You guys are awesome, and if you are reading this book, then you have journeyed with me for a while now, and I can't thank you enough for the honor.

Be sure to keep an eye out for the next installment in the Dragons of Daegonlot series! Although I'm not yet sure of the title, I do believe it will be the last book in the series, and we will finally have a conclusion to Daxon and Drakthira's journey. Til next time…

Made in the USA
Columbia, SC
23 November 2017